# Border of Vengeance

## By Daniel Byram

i

*Daniel Byram*

*Border of Vengeance*

Sierra West Books
PO Box 8835
Mesa, Arizona 85214

Second Edition - Print

Randy Lewis - Senior Editor
Art - public domain

ISBN-13: 978-1-892798-24-4

Author's note

This project began with the discovery of an old McClellan saddle at an antique store in Arizona. It was suggested to me at that time, that the saddle was a very good deal. I ended up buying it.

I also bought into a fascination with the horse cavalry. My new found hobby of collecting horse cavalry equipment (expensive) and researching old stories (not quite as expensive) led me from Fort Huachuca, Arizona to Fort Riley Kansas, to the stone foundations of Camp Slaughter. I found a few forgotten memoirs here, a few lost military journals there, and the next thing I knew, I had a file cabinet full of stories to share.

I made it my personal quest to assemble this information I discovered into a book. Although I have taken artistic license with some of the events, I hope to preserve the sense of adventure and daring which existed on the Arizona frontier circa 1910. My mission was to generate interest in this era and Cochise County in an entertaining way.

At the end of the book, I have provided historical notes and an additional reading list for those who wish to continue the adventure.

Thank you,

*Daniel Byram*

*Daniel Byram*

**Border of Vengeance**

# Prologue

## November 12, 1951 - Fort Huachuca, Arizona

Again, it was time to bury the dead. The old
man settled his thin frame back into the soft
leather car seat and gently leaned his head against
the fogged window of the large black Chrysler, the
cold glass providing some comfort for the mild
headache he had been suffering since he
awakened. His thoughts wandered as he stared out
over the rolling hills of Cochise County, pondering
who of his old friends were better off. Those who
passed before the end of the horses, or those few
who lingered long after the horses were gone?
Was it better to end life with honor and glory on
the field of battle, dying in your prime? Or to just
sit in a small room passing time and waiting for
the inevitable end... Helplessly observing the end
of the horse cavalry... Forced to stand by on the
sidelines, pushed out of the way of progress...
watching the coming of age of a mechanized
army... and to meekly endure failing health and
the humiliations that come with old age?

As the big car turned toward the main gate of
Fort Huachuca, he wiped the glass with his gloved
hand, stealing a glimpse of the outside, looking to

the North at the foothills of the Whetstone Mountains. His eyes grew tired and he closed them for just a moment. His mind drifted to the beginning of it all, back to his first battle, back to Cuba.

### Cuba - June 30, 1898

The young Captain drew a deep breath, and then forced himself to open his eyes. It was time to assess the damage. Fighting the urge to keep his eyes closed tight, and summoning what courage he could, he first took a quick peek at the damage, before forcing himself to make a closer examination of his leg wound. Strangely, there was no sense of pain, not like he expected, just a throbbing ache and a vague feeling of disconnection. None of it seemed real. He could sense himself being overwhelmed, swept away from reality with a feeling of detachment, a remoteness swirling through him as though he was looking down at someone else. He slowly lifted his head and stared down to find dark blood flowing out a large black hole... a grizzly puncture wound through his calf. The damage appeared severe enough that getting to his feet and continuing the fight would be hopeless. He started to feel a sense of panic, fear crawling like a maggot into his stomach and chest, filling his head, pushing out rational thought. He might lose the leg. He might die.

The Captain took another breath, then a deeper one, calming himself, struggling to focus as he studied the wound. He could not see bone but the meat was torn below his knee so deeply that it looked like he could put his entire finger in the hole. He reached down with his left hand and tried it. He touched something, something foreign in the wound. He thought he could feel the metal fragment buried at a depth between his knuckle and the first joint of his finger.

Had he been knocked unconscious? How long? He wasn't sure, it felt as though he had just awakened from a deep sleep, experiencing intense vivid dreams, but this was real. He fought to focus. He began to hear men moaning, sporadic rifle fire, and he smelled gunpowder, smoke, and blood. Reality began forcing its way into his reverie. Sounds and smells of battle grew louder.

His thoughts remained cloudy... the attack must have failed. He shook his head and blinked... What happened? The outset of the assault remained clear in his mind, and then the burning pain of a round fired from a Spanish fortification. It hit him in the right upper chest, disabling his arm... now hanging numb and useless. He watched men fall... many men, dying as they charged into the initial volleys from the Spanish fortifications.

Then the worst happened. The line began to break. Failure was imminent... Collapse of the assault... Certain death.

In spite of the chest wound, he had tried to rally the men but chaos reigned, the intense fire raining down relentlessly from the hill... too intense. Then, as he stood over the bodies of the fallen troops, shouting unheard words of encouragement at his retreating men, another round from the Spanish troops struck his leg and he collapsed with the rest... into the pile of the dead and dying.

Failure... The attack was repelled.... His men... Where were they? All he could see was bodies.

He shook his head... pushing the humiliation of defeat out of his mind, and forcing himself to concentrate on survival.

I cannot bring back the dead. I have to move forward, he thought. Regroup the survivors, prepare to repel a counter attack... This fight is not over... get up.... What is happening now?

He had to see. He had to fight. With the last measure of his strength, he tried to lift his revolver, but it was heavy, almost too heavy to point. He thumbed back the hammer and squeezed the trigger, the barrel aimed in the direction of the fortifications. Click.

He groaned in frustration... Am I the last Officer? My God... Am I the last man?

His instinctive drive to fight faded as he succumbed to the reality that none of it really mattered any more. No final shot at the enemy... not even a last round saved for himself. His ammunition was gone, his men all dead.

The combined effects of blood loss and dense clouds of gunpowder and dust began to distort his view, producing a surreal vision of the battlefield. He tried to focus his eyes but he nearly exhausted the last of his strength with the effort of blinking, his eyes heavy, trying to clarify the scene... Death was imminent.

There were craters everywhere. Bodies sprawled across the hill. He could hear small artillery fire. *Theirs or ours?* It did not matter.

The grass, dark green only hours before, was so stained with blood that it took on a reddish brown tint. He took a last look at the corpses of gallant men strewn about him, littering the slopes. Men he led, many of them he considered friends... people he cared about... knew... all dead. His torment heightened with the descent of flies and jungle insects.... scavengers, carrying out the

5

natural order of things.

It was over.... done... lost...

The wounded officer saw something... movement... or was it? He was unable to determine if the visions before him were real, or if his senses, distorted by pain and blood loss, were now simply torturing him with horrible delusions of hell.

The Captain stared toward the enemy position, squinting into the sun setting over the hill between him and the Spanish fortification. A small squad of the enemy's infantry closed, approaching the slight depression in the ground in which he was lying. They moved forward cautiously, bayonets fixed. The soldiers were carefully searching the battlefield, stepping over the American bodies, thrusting cold steel into anyone showing signs of life. Stealing what they could find of value from the dead... cowards coming down from the hill after the battle to dispatch the wounded. No prisoners would be taken today. No survivors left to tell their tale of misadventure, a failed attack that was probably hopeless to begin with, another failed gesture of gallantry in a pointless war.

The helpless officer looked around as the enemy approached. The others were dead. He was alone. He stared at his friends' bodies and imagined he would soon be with them. He rolled to his left to turn his eyes away from the oncoming soldiers, seeking peace with a short prayer for his soul and the souls of his fallen comrades, waiting for a bayonet thrust in the back. If he could only get to his feet, he could die like a man.

Shots... renewed gunfire snapped him back from his dark musings. Shapes were winding through the mist. He tried to focus. Rescuers? He saw two hulks, and with the desperate renewal of hope in a hopeless situation, he strained to make them out. American sergeants, one black and one white, cut from the same mold, each at least six feet tall and over well over two hundred pounds, big men moving quickly. With pistols in each hand and more pistols jammed in their belts they sprinted towards the wounded officer, dodging fire and leaping over obstacles, bodies, and craters with the grace of mountain goats yet with the fierce determination of charging grizzlies.

The Captain couldn't signal or cry out, he could only watch as a desperate race began with him as the prize, six of the enemy, cowards who were executing the wounded, against the two American sergeants, beastly men, savage warriors looking for blood. As the men closed, he could suddenly see every drop of sweat on their faces with a

7

clarity he had never experienced before. Although they seemed to be moving slowly, with dreamlike motion, they were sprinting across the field of battle shouting their war screams like bloodthirsty jackals. With each stride across the sloping field of dead men, the Sergeants lifted and fired pistols. With cracks like thunder, the smoke and flame rolled gracefully out of the barrels. The enemy troops who had come down from the hill to murder the wounded began to fall.

A shot ripped through the uniform above the hip of the large black man but did not slow him down. The Sergeants were showing teeth, a hateful snarl distorting their faces. Mucous, sweat, and blood ran down their fierce blistered faces. The inhuman war screams of his rescuers frightened even the Captain. He saw the horrible visage of total war personified. Death, rampaging with a bloody glee, slaying enemies, and drenched in an aura of purity only the true warrior knows... the joy that exists in a fight to the death.

The enemy soldiers drew nearer, moving and firing. A round ripped a small furrow in the ground near the officer but he did not react. He was enchanted with the brutal fight for ownership of his life... he could merely wait, uninvolved, observing as a detached soul might look down on its dead earthly body.

The 'whump' of beef striking beef exploded over him as four of the enemy collided with the two rescuers in mortal conflict. Too close for gunfire, bayonets and daggers flashed, stabbing, hacking, and chopping through flesh in bloody combat over the Captain laying helplessly on the ground. Warm blood splashed over his face, as blades were jammed through meat and into vital organs. The captain could only lay on the ground and watch as the black Sergeant standing over him choked the life out of a man with his massive right arm while using his free hand to strike another enemy in face with a pistol butt sending teeth and a piece of lip flying. He heard a man...somewhere... screaming before dying. Who was it? The disgusting crunch of broken bones preceded the descent of the limp body of the choked man into the pile of the dead.

The white Sergeant used a bayonet and his fists on three foes. Stabbing and punching, he ignored the pain of a butt stroke to his right shoulder that would have killed a normal man. He turned long enough to kick the man in the stomach and deliver a hammering fist to the back of his head. Blood exploded out of the man's mouth, nose, and ears from the force of the strike, the single blow instantly fatal.

The Captain could only lie there and watch as more blood was spilled over him from the fight. Not drips, but splashes... Horrible wounds... lethal wounds were inflicted. More bodies fell. Finally, a grunt... a snapped neck... and the last enemy soldier collapsed. The only other men left alive in the little hollow were to the two American Sergeants standing over him.

The Captain winced in pain from his wounds when he felt tug of the Sergeants pulling him out of the pile of dead men. One of them addressed him in a heavy Irish brogue, "Will there be anything else we can do for the Captain, sir?" He smiled pleasantly although covered in gunpowder and gore, his uniform torn... the ruddy face, big and wide.

"Lets just get out of here, for God's sake," the Captain rasped. He sensed the last bit of his consciousness slipping away. All that he could make out of the face in front of him was the two bushy red eyebrows.

The officer heard another voice, a heavy drawl of the Deep South, but not speaking to him. The voice, a gravelly baritone, was challenging the hulking Irishman. "Sergeant Bronk, for once would you follow orders and do as the Captain says? I ain't inclined to be waiting around here all day for you to decide whether or not you want to do as your told. Not like the last time. You being a stubborn mic is gonna get us all killed."

The officer opened his eyes and saw a large black man now leaning over him. He heard the man addressing the red headed Sergeant, who did not appear to be paying attention to him. He was busying himself, scanning the horizon for additional hostile forces and reloading a pistol. The big Irishman's twisted smile and fiery blue eyes gave the appearance that he was not thinking about finding a safe place to retreat to. The man was hoping for another fight.

Suddenly, the white Sergeant seemed to freeze as he processed his partner's comment. He stopped what he was doing, stood up straight, and turned slowly, placing his hands on his hips and snorting, "What do you mean 'for once' you fat tub of manure. I always follow orders. You're the one who is the most insubordinate son-of-a-bitch I ever knew in this man's army." He argued defensively before pausing to look back down at the wounded Captain to offer an explanation, "At least I never hit an officer."

The black Sergeant closed with him eye to eye, "Well why don't you try and kick my insubordinate ass then you gutless, whiskey breath, bag of potato growing wind?" The black Sergeant got even closer, touching nose to nose, accepting the Irishman's challenge. Neither man gave an inch.

The wounded Captain considered the possibility that since these two had killed everyone else, they were now going to fight each other. Men of violence require conflict to survive… its an addiction that has no cure. The Captain's could now only utter a hoarse whisper, "Sergeants, the matter of the war."

Another round tore through a bloody mud puddle near their feet splashing debris into their faces. The captain collapsed, losing consciousness.

When he woke up in a field hospital three days later, his last recollection of the incident was being grabbed under the arms and hauled away by the grizzlies… two hulking bears dragging a prize back to their lair.

## Fort Huachuca

The car hit a pothole in the narrow road. The sudden impact jarring the old man awake, bringing his thoughts back to the present. The aging soldier slowly opened his eyes as the car passed slowly past the parade field and turned west. The cemetery, concealed in a narrow valley, was accessible only by a one lane road winding through mesquite covered hills. A black iron gate shrouded the entry to a field of white stones. The grounds were grass covered but the turf was turning brown with the coming of winter. The threatening thunderheads rolled over the hilltops allowing only filtered light to penetrate the ceremony.

The lonely valley outside Fort Huachuca, Arizona would be the resting place of a brave man. At the graveside stood an honor detail and a handful of mourners, most of whom were church people from the post, volunteering to provide the illusion of family. Only the old man was a comrade in arms of the deceased.

He leaned on his cane and maintained a stoic presence over the grave of his friend, but his steely veneer finally cracked at the sixth note of taps. The weathered face, pitted by dust storms and scarred in combat, at last gave way to an expression of realization. He suddenly recognized the finality of not only a man, but also a part of their way of life. The sad gray eyes of the old soldier wept.

The ancient veteran knew that his turn to rest would soon come. No one else present at the service would quietly reflect on the glory, the heartache, the joy, or even the times of terror that were part of life on the Arizona border. No one would laugh or cry at the recollections of the good times and the hard times of soldiering together in the United States Cavalry. He was the last man. The best he could hope when it was his turn was for was the camp volunteers to make an appearance, dutifully mourning someone they never knew.

There were no sentiments he could express today over the grave of a good man that would mean anything to anyone present. So, when it was his turn to give a eulogy, he spoke for his comrades waiting at Fiddler's Green, the mythological resting place of cavalrymen. "Heavenly Father… let my friend's worldly remains rest here on this sacred ground with his saber. But for his spirit, I pray that he may have a camp by fresh water, tall grass, the company of good men, and fine horses. And may he buy the first drink when we are all together again. Lord, I don't believe he was much of a Christian, but if you can find mercy for a good soldier and a damned fine horseman, I would be obliged."

The brief ceremony ended and the group carelessly disassembled. They left the old man, leaning on his cane, mourning alone as they slowly returned to their cars.

A young Corporal from the honor guard waited

outside the cemetery gates for the old man. He awkwardly approached the Colonel in a way that a man does when he knows he should not be bothering someone, but he must… or he will never get the opportunity again. He took a forceful step, then slowed, took a smaller step while getting the courage to approach the old soldier like a man… respectfully, but cautiously.

The corporal cleared his throat, and asked, "Sir, I know this isn't the time sir, but… I understand that you served in the horse cavalry, and… I was hoping there would be a chance to speak to you about it sometime. I'd really like to know what it was like, who these men were." He pointed to the fresh grave.

The old man halted his shuffling abruptly. He turned, looking up into the face at the apologetic young soldier. He had already wiped the tears away from his weathered face with a wool gloved hand. He gave the young man the stare that had once made troopers shake a lifetime ago on the Arizona frontier. It burned through the soldier like molten lead blazing from the barrel of an '03' Springfield 30-06.

The young soldier, surprised at the ancient man's intensity, stumbled back a step as though he had been shot. "Sir, I am so sorry, I just didn't know if you would ever be here again and… I'm sorry, I know it was inappropriate of me to bother you."

The old man could see the young soldier was thoroughly embarrassed. He watched intently as the Corporal made an awkward attempt at turning away and abandoning his inquiry, but the old man's stare held him there, transfixed as a moth to a flame, with his gray eyes. He sized the young man up one more time.

The old man let the stare burn… just long enough. He always had a sense of timing about things like that. It was good to know he still had the gift.

The Colonel spoke softly, "You're wrong mister… this may well be the right time to share this story. But there will be one thing in return that I will ask of you."

The soldier agreed to the terms.

# Chapter 1

### Arizona Territory - May 3, 1911

The rider leaned slightly forward in the McClellan saddle and squeezed with his legs. He could feel the long legged bay explode from a trot to a high lope. Following the sandy desert wash, he let the horse stretch out and run as the rider carefully released pressure of the bit and gave him his head. The flying hooves kicked up a spray of sand behind the horse as they ran. After half of a mile, the rider relaxed in the saddle and whispered, "Easy" then gave a slight touch to the reins and quickly released. The horse slowed. The rider again touched the reins just hard enough for slight contact with the horse's mouth and repeated the command, "easy." He could feel the big Thoroughbred-Morgan horse relax and effortlessly glide into a trot. After a quarter mile to cool down, they slowed to a fast walk.

The switchback trail they followed began at the base of the wash and led to the top of a small hill north of Douglas, Arizona. From the top of the hill, the man had a commanding view of the Cavalry camp. He could also see a large section of the road that crossed the Southeastern part of Cochise County, Arizona connecting the San Bernardino Valley to the Mining town of Bisbee. In the clear morning air, he could make out the hills of Mexico in the distance.

The man stepped down from the saddle and loosened the cinch. He quickly checked each hoof for stones or a loose shoe. He gently stroked the horse's neck before reaching into the black saddle bag and finding one of his cigars and a wooden match.

He untied a knot with a quick tug and loosened the lead rope from around the horse's neck. He tethered his mount to a Palo Verde tree and then found his favorite boulder to perch on while he enjoyed the day, his cigar, and the view.

His horse, sensing it was time to rest, let out a relaxed snort and munched on Palo Verde leaves and whatever dry desert grass was within range of his lead rope.

Camp Harry T. Jones was a place as isolated from the hubbub of the War Department in Washington as a good soldier could find. The man knew many of his peers questioned his desire to command of a cavalry outpost and remount station located on the Mexican border in the God forsaken territory of Arizona. Jones was the last place you would look for promotion, or civilized living, but the man knew it was a damned good place to find trouble, and dealing with trouble was

what soldiers were for. He didn't accept a
commission to attend fancy balls and state dinners
in the safe confines of Washington D.C.

He looked over his right shoulder to the
Dragoon Mountains. A few miles northwest was
the infamous boomtown of Tombstone, although
in 1910, it was more of a ghost town than an
infamous mining camp. Still, raiding bandits and
renegade Indians kept things interesting for the
adventurous souls populating the area. The town
of Bisbee, twenty miles west Northwest of the
camp was now booming as a mining town, its
sudden wealth bringing desperadoes, outlaws and
riffraff from both sides of the border to the ethnic
mixture of immigrant workers and entrepreneurs

Arizona would do just fine until the next real
war beckoned him. The desert had a harshness
tempered by a physical beauty, the smells, the
sounds, were part of the visual experience. It was
alive, beautiful, and dangerous at the same time.

As the man surveyed the area he called his
command, he took a long drag on the Cuban cigar.
Slowly he exhaled a cloud of smoke and watched it
drift away in the light breeze that seemed to
always prevail from the West. The high desert of
Cochise County was cooler than Tucson by about
five to ten degrees and provided a livable summer

and a mild winter, but that was where the pleasantry ended. He looked across the panorama at the valleys divided with rambling, rocky mountain ranges: the Chiricahua, the Dragoon, and the Whetstone. Survival in the high desert depended on an ability to adapt.

He heard his horse exhale deeply, snorting a relaxed sound. The horses here were special. He considered the difference in the mounts he used in Kansas at Fort Riley as compared to the horses suitable to this rugged land. Here, a horse had to have rock feet and the agility of a big horn sheep to survive in the mountains. Horses without those attributes sooner or later found themselves as dinner for mountain lions.

This beautiful but harsh land held lessons for a man as well. A man soldiering on the border frontier had to learn to survive rattle snakes, scorpions and other men; those men with the predatory tendencies of the wolf, the occasional Yaqui raiding party, border robbers, ambushers, and just plain mean bastards who hunted the hills of southern Arizona. Not unlike the coyote that hunts small rabbits or mice, they searched for weakness, found it, and killed it. Colonel R. J. Mason knew that for the people of the border country, weakness meant death, unless a protector could be found.

## Four miles Northeast of Nogales

The stocky, roman-nosed paint horse hung its head in fatigue in the desert wash, too tired to nibble at the leaves on the Mesquite tree he was tied to. A gaunt man lay prone on the slight rise nearby. He was nearly invisible on the desert floor in his faded canvas pants and dirty white cotton shirt. An experienced desert man, he wore his sleeves long in spite of the heat to protect himself from the sun. He placed his model 94 Winchester 30-30 rifle in front of him as he reached around his side for the case containing the telescope. He rubbed the dust from his right eye and raised the instrument to view the source of the black smoke he noted a few miles back as he trailed his quarry, a two bit Mexican bandit named Juan Pedro Garcia. He focused the telescope on a burning building. He could make out a ranch house, apparently deserted. He strained to see the details then looked away in disgust and horror, more bodies.

He glassed the entire area, confirming the outlaws were long gone. He raised himself to one knee and brushed off his clothes. The horseman picked up his rifle and walked back to the wash. He cursed aloud as he placed the telescope back in the case, shoved the rifle in the scabbard, and secured his equipment to his saddle. He rationed himself a small sip of water out of his canteen, then wetted his fingers and rubbed them on the paint horses grateful lips.

Placing a foot in the stirrup, he hoisted himself into the saddle and slowly road to the smoldering ranch house.

"We're farther behind the son-of-a-bitch than I thought, Tex." He spoke softly to his horse as the tired animal plodded towards the smoky remains.

The rider mumbled, "Whoa," and touched the reins lightly bringing the horse to a stop. He reached in his saddlebag and pulled out a small metal star. He rubbed the dirt off of it and read the worn inscription engraved on the surface, Arizona Ranger. He pinned it to his shirt and gave the horse a slight squeeze with his knees, cuing him to walk again toward the ranch.

The ranger grimly rode to the body of a man hanging from the limb of a tree. The tips of the man's toes nearly touched the ground. The ranger spoke out loud, "Goddam, the poor bastard must have strangled on this limb instead of getting a quick broken neck from a clean hanging." He stepped off the horse and examined the body. He spun it around to see the face and took a sharp step back in shock. The eyelids had been cut off and the matter left in the eye sockets was thick with flies. One blue pupil was still recognizable as a human eye, staring into the face of the ranger.

"Dammit... You butchers!" He shouted as he spun away and kicked at the dirt in frustration. A black thought came over him as he realized the eyelids were cut off to force the man to watch something, but what?

The ranger walked through the rubble that was left of the ranch and found the bodies, a woman and a young girl, violated and then mutilated horribly. The ranger had no wife or children, but he was raised with little sisters who he cherished, not much older than this girl when he saw them last. What kind of man was Garcia? The terror the woman and the little girl must have faced in death was beyond the limits the Ranger could imagine. He fell to his knees and cried out in rage, an unintelligible scream of hatred.

He looked south and raised a fist to the sky. The ranger vowed to the setting sun, "You dirty bastards are damned sure going to die for this, you thieving, murdering cowards."

His rage vented, he slumped to his knees in resignation, accepting that revenge would have to come another day. The Ranger went about the grim business of cutting the dead man down and burying the family. He found dirt soft enough to dig west of the remains of the ranch house at what must have been a small garden before riders trampled it. He dug the graves with a piece of wood deep enough to discourage coyotes from digging them up. Working up a sweat, he gathered rocks to pile over the graves just in case they were not quite deep enough. He spoke words over the crude mounds the best he could.

His heart told him to pursue the outlaws. The trail was clear, but it went to Mexico. His mind told him to wait, get more help, and settle it when the bandits came back... they always came back. He heated some coffee over the still hot coals of the ranch house to rest his horse before going back to Tucson. He would be ready next time.

**Agua Prieta, Mexico - May 5, 1911**

The stone building and makeshift bar was crowded with soldiers and local cowboys. The drinking began in earnest during the early afternoon and had not slowed by sunset.

The big American soldier with stripes on his sleeve raised a glass of tequila as he loudly proposed a toast with his thick Irish brogue, "To the greatest holiday of them all, Saint Patrick's Day."

A vaquero tossed his glass on the floor,

punctuating the act by spitting on the floor. "Maybe you don't know but this is Mexico, my amigo, and today we only toast Cinco De Mayo, what you gringos would call our Independence Day. No one here gives a damn about this saint of yours."

The soldier finished his drink and slowly set the glass on the bar and sought clarification, "I'm beggin' your complete pardon, sir, but did I see you spit on the floor at the conclusion of my toast?"

The Mexican cowboy, a big heavy set man, stepped back from the bar, "Gringo, let me explain this one more time... Uno mas. I spit on the floor, I spit on you, and I spit on your pinchi uniform too!"

The group of cowboys snickered at the insult, muttering more profanities in support of their friend.

The big soldier wrinkled his brow as the barroom patrons slowly divided themselves into two distinct groups, soldiers or cowboys. Everyone in the bar knew what was going to happen. A fight was coming. Sides were chosen. It was only a matter of who would throw the first punch.

The soldier growled as he got nose to nose with the cowboy, "I'll be acceptin' your apology, laddie. Obviously you've had too much to drink and it's ruined your good judgment."

The cowboy spit on the soldier's left boot in reply.

The big man smiled.

**May 6, 1911 at 4:30AM**

A morning bugle call pierced the glaring headache like a bayonet, arousing around two hundred and fifty pounds of semi-conscious ugly man. Flatulence resembling the sound of a tuba player warming up for a parade, a sour belch, and a little head shake were the only indications that the bulging lump on the bunk was alive. The last loud fart smelled so foul that the huddled mass pulled his head out from under the blanket and sucked down a deep breath of fresh air.

Bronk, the top Sergeant of B Troop, raised his bulk to the edge of his bunk and squeezed his pounding head with both hands to keep it from exploding all over the tent. "As God is my witness, I shall never drink again... in that God forsaken country of Mexico." He paused, and then decided to be safe and qualify his hangover oath, "On that cursed day of sinkhole tomato." As the tent spun slowly around in a nauseating circle, Bronk attempted to sort out what happened the night before at the local celebration of Cinqo De Mayo.

Now, although too late, he realized he should not have listened to the troopers advising him earlier in the week when they said Cinco De Mayo was essentially a Mexican Saint Patty's Day. It was clearly some kind of heathen celebration. Tequila was usually involved. But how could he had forgotten, this being the fifteenth year in a row he made the same mistake.

Bronk burped, and then remembered having left the camp early the preceding day on his personal mount 'Mac' a bulky 14-3 hand high chunky built bay gelding that was also nearly 14-3 hands wide. They rode across the border to celebrate with the Mexican locals. Old Mac, he recalled accusingly, was more than willing to carry his partner down to the celebration and his demise. Bronk moaned aloud, "I can't believe me old 'harse' Mac would have the poor judgment to let me get into something like that."

Bronk massaged his temples, ineffectively trying to relieve the pain, as he sat on the edge of his bunk. He recalled crossing the line into Agua Prieta, Mexico with only the best intentions. He made a feeble attempt at self delusion... finally concluding that it was his patriotic duty to show the locals how an Irish-Polish-American celebrates the national holiday of his forbears.

27

Bronk looked at the floor of his tent and woefully moaned, "That cursed tequila!"

There had been a lot of tequila the night before. He remembered something about trouble evolving from the drinking that led to an unfortunate misunderstanding and some kind of minor brawl.

Bronk rubbed his jaw. The Sergeant cursed under his breath as more details of the incident came back to him. There was definitely a scuffle of some type. He wondered, as he moved about the tent, preparing for the day, "Why do these unfortunate situations always seemed to happen to me?" he muttered.

Bronk answered himself as he pulled on his blouse, "It's that cursed Latin machismo. *That* is what led that poor vaquero to resort to violence. Thank God at least I demonstrated the courtesy to be a gentlemen about it."

As he dressed and his stomach growled, the recollections became clearer. The honor of the unit, and Ireland had been called into question by the cowboys, and when honor is on the line, well, that is never a time to pull punches.

Bronk splashed some water in his face and the night's activities finally started becoming clear.

The first punch in the fight was Bronk's. Like a huge boulder launched from a catapult, Bronk's big fist connected and the vaquero's jaw met the force of an Army mule's kick. That cowboy was no longer a factor in the fight, but he was not alone. When the limp figure of the fighting vaquero crashed with a dull thud face first on the floor, the other cowboys swarmed Bronk.

Before the first chair could be broken over Bronk's head, the men of "B" Troop leaped to action to defend their Sergeant. Bronk felt like the object of a tug-of war between cowboys and cavalry. They struggled like terriers pulling a rat out of a burrow. More men piled on and the fight was soon out of control and spilling into the street. Punches and kicks were exchanged in the mass of combatants. Eventually, the Americans retrieved their leader from the melee and began a tactical retreat to the U.S. border.

Bronk had not been so drunk that he forgot the pursuit home. He still felt the sore on his back from an object hitting him as the cowboys threw bottles, sticks, and rocks at the Norte Americanos as they were chased out of Mexico and back into Douglas, Arizona. Bronk smiled as he remembered old Mac trampling on a slow moving cowboy in a sombrero during the informal deportation procedures, not enough to hurt him, but enough to maintain a healthy respect for the Americans, or at least their horses.

Bronk remembered being dragged back to his quarters by about ten of the troopers, preventing him from going back into Mexico to finish the fight. One of the older troops had mentioned something about Bronk escalating a small misunderstanding into an international incident.

Bronk considered the whole matter as a personal affront. He tried to rally the retreating soldiers for a full scale invasion of Mexico but the consensus of the soldiers, and probably the vaqueros too, was they had all the invasion they needed for one evening.

His fellow soldiers had unceremoniously dumped Bronk through the flaps of his tent.

Having sorted out the circumstances of his current feeling of general discomfort, the old Sergeant stood up and stretched. Today was another workday and the fun was over for now, or at least until next payday.

He straightened his blouse, imbibed in a brief snort of the hair of the dog from a small metal flask, and made for the door.

At five in the morning, with only two hours sleep, even the faint light of dawn made Bronk stop and blink.

"Good morning, Top. Having a bout of the flu

today?" Corporal Blue asked, still sore from dragging Bronk back to camp. Blue was amazed that the Sarge was not being hauled to the infirmary instead of marching briskly to the stables.

"Nothing a good cigar and a puke won't cure laddie." Bronk stomped his feet to start his circulation and pulled a fine large Cuban cigar out of his blouse. He had developed a taste for them following the campaign in Havana. He made a display of smelling the cigar, passing it under his nose.

Blue challenged Bronk on the source of the smoke, "Sarge, where the hell do you get those fancy cigars? I know you don't buy them on a sergeant's pay."

Bronk took a deep breath and slowly exhaled like a frustrated teacher mentoring a dull student. "Ever since I single-handedly saved their bloody island in '98, the King of Cuba sends me as many as I want. I'm like a son to him, I am." Bronk paused and slowly leaned forward into Blue's face if on the verge of whispering a secret, then shouted at the top of his lungs, "Now get out of me way you nosy little man!" causing Blue to stumble backward and fall awkwardly on his butt.

Bronk marched past Blue and strode through

the open doors of the main barn like a conquering barbarian. He walked to the rear of the stables to have his puke. That bit of unpleasantness out of the way, he returned to the remuda and struck another match off the beard of Corporal Schmidt. He lit his Havana and savored the taste of the fine cigar. He addressed the corporal, obviously delighting in the sound of his own thick Irish brogue, "Smitty me boy, on this fine day, could you please form a detail of the gentlemen from the guardhouse to haul this horse shit out of here? Remember to take a wagon load to Mrs. Lopez's house for her vegetable garden."

"Sarge, the Lieutenant doesn't like us hauling horse shit off the camp. He says it's a waste of time and it really seems to piss him off. He says military horse shit is for military use only and shouldn't be issued to civilians."

Bronk absorbed this bit of military logic and exhaled a cloud of cigar smoke. As the smoke cloud lingered in the air above his head, he stared up at it, as if expecting to see the answer to a philosophical question magically appear in the mist. He tucked his chin, wrinkled his brow, and increased the volume of his speech substantially causing Schmidt to lean backwards.

"Young Corporal, I don't remember bringing

this matter up to a blasted vote. You can either get those drunken jackasses out of the guard shack and down to the stables, or start shoveling shit yourself you argumentative little kraut! Now please see to it before I kick your sorry arse."

The conversation ended with a muttered, "Yes, Sergeant." Schmidt did an about face and walked off to take charge of the poor prisoners for a day of hard labor. Bronk placed his thumbs under his suspenders and lifted them off his chest as he deeply inhaled the brisk morning air. He couldn't help but feel good. It was a beautiful day, he had a fine cigar, and he had dispensed justice to those lecherous captives in the guard shack who had been foolish enough to engage in disruptive behavior and then let themselves be caught. Most of all, he was unduly pleased with himself for using the magic word 'please' to get a job done. How could Second Lieutenant Cleary find me to be coarse and unreasonable now?" He asked himself. "Ah yes, today will be a lovely day, indeed."

*Daniel Byram*

## Chapter 2

Second Lieutenant Cleary, an academy man, had never visited any of the civilized land west of the Mississippi before he found himself living on the wild and remote Mexican border. He hated the West. Before this posting, everything was different... good... happy... Now life seemed pointless.

Cleary sat dejectedly in his tent, lamenting his assignment at Camp Jones, cursing the general who sent him here. In the dim light of dawn, he squinted while entering a note in his journal, *'The men are filthy undisciplined pigs, the camp is a disaster, and the Arizona Territory is more barren and ugly than hell itself. I find the local people to be insipid and primitive. The unprepossessing lot of them do not justify the expense of military protection. I believe we would be best served letting the Mexican army serve these ingrates, dullards, and heathens.'*

Cleary, being the type of man who enjoyed the discipline and the refined social order of 'The Point,' anguished over being sent to the frontier and the certainty of a premature end to what should have been a glorious military, and probably political career. He thought about the fine mahogany desks, fine uniforms and Washington dinner parties. He continued writing, *'I can't comprehend what I've done or who I might have aggrieved, to be consigned to such a dismal fate as I find here in this God forsaken land of Arizona.'*

His disappointment in the assignment was compounded by his disgust with the men. As he wrote in his journal, he could only describe them as being *'nearly as savage as the hostile Indians who they claim once freely roamed the land. Although, from the looks of the Indians on the reservation, they couldn't have been too tough to tame McGuillicotty.* He added a notation summarizing his inspection that morning... the uniform appearance of the troops was sloppy, they are prone to excessive drinking, and they seemed to have a bizarre loyalty to that brutish, dim-witted Irish Top Sergeant.

Cleary looked up from his writing and slowly put his pen and journal down. He had an epiphany. "That must be it!"

Cleary thought about it, and made another note. 'It must be intimidation on that damnable Sergeant's part, with his foul vocabulary of vile opprobrium unleashed upon the men with alarming frequency. No wonder they are loyal, they are simply intimidated by their crude and undisciplined NCO.

Cleary now knew the truth. It was going to be up to him now to show these men what the regular Army was all about. He would make a point of straightening out that obnoxious mic sergeant at his earliest opportunity. Dressing him down properly for his crude manner of communicating with the men... it would be a pleasure. And the icing on the cake would be issuing a scathing reprimand to the sergeant in the presence of the troops. Maybe even a demotion... if that stubborn Colonel cooperates.

For the first time since his arrival in Arizona, Cleary felt good about things. He had calculated an opportunity to show the men that *he* was sympathetic towards them, thus winning their respect and admiration... and finally putting that despicable hulking sergeant in his proper place,. It would be glorious. Clearly could now establish himself as the boss. He closed the journal.

"I'll square that brute away, West Point style," he muttered to no one... he needed no one.

The Commander's Tent - Camp Jones

The tall lean officer tugged on his gloves as he paused outside the entrance to his tent. He was no longer young, but he still moved like a young man, typical of the aging outdoorsman breed of western male. He was a man comfortable in his position, living where he wanted to be, doing what he wanted to do.

He inhaled deeply, taking in a lung full of the dry desert air, sensing the odor of the horses, the creosote bush, and the mesquite. Colonel Raymond Jacob Mason marched out to the stables striding across the compound with that certain subtle swagger of the man in charge.

Mason's uniform was starched and immaculate. The campaign hat was eased over the at an angle matching that of his squinting left eye. The tilt of the hat gave him the tenor of a man looking for a fight. His pristine uniform suggested the possibility of a dilettante officer, but closer inspection sabotaged any impression of weakness. Under the leather gloves were scarred and gnarled hands. This officer's hands had broken noses, shod horses, and built forts,. They were not the hands of a man who spent a career shuffling memos and writing reports.

Mason had a reputation as the rare type of officer who did not require a position of rank to enjoy the loyalty of his command. HIs men would follow him to the worst parts of hell on his word alone that a job was there to be done and the privilege of enjoying a beer in the company of the old man at the end of a campaign.

Known as R.J. to his few friends, the boys in the troops reverently referred to him as *Old Mase.*

Although getting older, he was still a damned fine horseman. In his late fifties, he still moved as gingerly as a man at the prime of his life. With his confident stride and straight back, he could probably pass for a man of forty if one did not look too closely the weather beaten face that vaguely resembled a worn out saddlebag. The lines were not merely the result of aging skin, but years of desert campaigning, the wind, the heat, and Sonoran sun taking its toll.

Colonel Mason loved serving on the border. To some officers this kind of service meant isolation, but to Mason it was freedom; freedom for a man to *really* command. Mason hated the petty nonsense of the War Department and the squabbling and groveling for promotions that was routinely tolerated in Washington. He found his heaven at Camp Jones, and had no wish to leave the wild country, good horses, and loyal men who served with on the border to simply primp and preen in Washington among the squabbling bureaucrats competing to become a Brigadier.

It was not always this way. Mason had been a family man early on during his career, content to find civilized postings and peaceful surroundings. But his happiness turned to tragedy. He lost them all in a tragic house fire while he was deployed to Cuba.

He was severely wounded in combat. He barely made it home alive, only to find that there was nothing or no one to come home to. He was alone and his family was gone. Maybe that is what drove him to isolation, why he found solace in the desert. He never recovered from the loss. It was a horrible memory he would carry throughout his life. But the desert was a salve to the wound.

As the Colonel entered the stable, his first observation was Bronk... Top Sergeant Bronkowski McKinley McGuillicotty leaning on the corral, smoking a stogie, and gazing over the herd of remounts.

Mason knew Bronk well enough to know he was not looking at looking at anything in particular. Bronk was reminiscing about the past.

"It's a hell of a day in the Cavalry when the Colonel has to beg for a goddamned cigar from a drunken Mic Sergeant." He barked.

Bronk jumped to attention, "Well, then don't beg, Colonel darling. Just get over here and strike a bloody match. You're certainly getting sensitive in your golden years, Sir." Bronk displayed his well practiced face of shock and dismay that never seemed to fool anyone.

"Golden years my ass. I'd like to know how you're getting these expensive cigars on Sergeant's pay." Mason accepted the Havana as he scolded his old friend.

Bronk simply ignored the comment. He held a great deal of respect for the required social gap between officers and NCOs and, as a consequence, would never consider mentioning to anyone about the source of his continuing supply of cigars, gifts from an officer he had once helped on an island far away. Nevertheless, Bronk thought it odd that the Colonel, even in private, never admitted to being the anonymous benefactor. The war in Cuba was hell, but what came after for Mason was worse. Bronk had stood by him there too.

Mason changed the subject. "How do the new horses look, Sergeant?" Colonel Mason pulled a match out of his shirt pocket and struck it across the adobe block wall, smoothly igniting the head as he then lit the cigar.

The question shook Bronk from his memories of Cuba and back to the present. "They're a fine lot this time, sir. Wild as marsh hares, but the boys can ride the rough off of them," he said confidently. "Morgans is what they are, Sir, nice stout bastards, the lot of them. I was just admiring the look of that chunky bay gelding over there." Bronk pointed across the corral with his cigar a wide backed chunky horse.

Mason looked over at the bay and thought that it resembled Mac, only a little skinnier. No wonder Bronk fancied it. "Those Morgans are a little short for my tastes but they certainly are big stout bastards, " Mason agreed as he took a puff on the cigar, enjoying the distinct aroma of the burning Cuban tobacco.

McGuillicotty growled at a private who passed by carrying a bucket, directing him to fetch and groom the colonel's personal mount. While they were waiting, the Colonel took a deep breath and carefully addressed his concern about a new officer at the camp.

"About Mr. Cleary, do you think you can straighten out that young Lieutenant, Top?" Colonel Mason purposely focused his gaze on the remounts to avoid seeing the ugly grimace on Top's gnarled face at the mention of the name of his relentless tormentor, Lieutenant Cleary.

"I certainly hope so, sir. He seems like a fine boy." Bronk suppressed the urge for another puke after spouting the preposterous lie.

"Well, the boy has decent breeding, but his

head is stuck so far up his ass that I fear he couldn't find the light of day at high noon," Mason muttered, "we desperately need good officers out here on the frontier, and I sincerely hope you can make him into one. He is all we have got to work with and he will have to do. It's a sergeant's duty, Bronk... do what you can."

"Aye, sir, a Sergeant's duty it is. I will certainly try my best, sir. Enjoy your ride, Colonel, " Bronk responded stiffly, now grumpy again at the prospect of being tasked with fixing Lieutenant Cleary.

"Thank you, Top," Mason checked the girth of the McClellan then stepped into the stirrup and threw a leg over the tall thoroughbred. Purposefully, he avoided any eye contact with Bronk. Mason rode off without any further discussion.

McGuillicotty cursed his luck. The bad luck of the Irish, having to fix another West Point boy wonder, and with him at this ripe old age, and with his health being so poor lately. Perhaps a little medicine would help. If memory served, Bronk recalled there might be a spare bottle of medicine hidden in the tack room. He glanced over his shoulder to confirm the Colonel was out of sight then went off to look.

*Daniel Byram*

# Chapter 3

## The Border

The communities of Douglas, Arizona and Agua Prieta, Sonora are twin border towns sharing common interests in commerce and similar populations, yet they are clearly divided by an imaginary line delineating political entities and their respective laws, or lack of laws. In 1910, problems rarely occurred on *El frontiere*, particularly among the local people. Most of the population remained on one side or the other of the border unless they made an exception for specific business or social purposes, and they had little interest or reason for causing trouble. To the observer, the obvious explanation to their limited interaction and conflict was that the folks who lived there were too tired from working like dogs just to survive. They seldom had strength left to cause any trouble. There was no energy for bickering, most people focused on limited options that the times afforded them... work, feeding their families, and sleeping.

Near the conjoined cities, was Camp Jones, situated on open range between the town of Douglas and the ranch of Texas John Slaughter.

Slaughter, a famous lawman during his prime,

was the former sheriff of Cochise County. Many county residents credited him with running the scum of West Texas out of Arizona, and finally ending the Clanton and Earp trouble of the early eighties. He was a tough old bastard who tolerated no foolishness. The aging Slaughter was respected throughout the region. The ranch, like most of the big spreads, was still operated by old man Slaughter and his family. The cattle and farming operation covered over one hundred thousand acres spanning both sides of the border. This led to occasional disputes with the political and military powers over the years. But whatever the problems of the past, the Slaughter family had been supportive of the US Army, although the support probably had more to do with keeping roving bands of rustlers out of Arizona than it did with sheer patriotism. Old man Slaughter was shrewd enough to know that cavalry activity on his ranch would encourage the border robbers to go bother someone else and leave his cattle alone.

The town of Douglas was filled with hard working miners, farmers, and shopkeepers. The new Gadsden Hotel had just opened on G Street and 11th. Its marble staircase and stained glass windows were a reflection of the riches brought in by the new smelters built for processing ore. The twin city on the South side of the border, Agua Prieta, shared the same class of hard working people who were enjoying the newfound prosperity of the modern age. Unfortunately, Agua Prieta, Mexico was more accessible to a new kind of vermin as well... the so-called revolutionaries who were popping up along all border towns. Most of these revolutionaries were common robbers and rustlers who used the excuse of oppression and poverty to legitimize their depredations.

Garcia was such a man. Juan Pedro was known to his associates as El Cuchillo, loosely translated as The Knife. A name given to him because of his reputation for cruelty and love of carving people like butchering animals. He routinely dismembered his enemies a piece at a time until they bled their lifeblood out on the ground before him. He enjoyed their screams. The sound of helpless people dying appealed to his sadistic nature.

After years of stealing cattle on the American side, and robbing innocent travelers on both sides of the border, Juan Pedro Garcia had politicized his activities, declaring himself a Villista, a devoted supporter of Francisco "Pancho " Villa.

Pancho Villa was just another random killer, terrorizing the countryside, who held an insatiable desire for political power in the unstable government of Mexico. The key difference between Villa and other organized criminals in the area was his fame. He had become a local folk hero to the peasants of northern Mexico as Zapata had to the South. His friend and protector, Ignacio Madero, a young idealistic attorney and leader of the resistance to President Diaz, fueled Villa's hatred for the government, and inspired his self-serving insurrection against Mexico with wild tales of fascism and dictatorships.

El Cuchillo had about fifteen riders at any given time, other misfits and blackguards, filthy criminals like himself who now rode with heads high in the name of Villa and the revolution. Accepting El Cuchillo's rhetoric, the outlaws who rode with him operated under the belief that their leader was an important officer in Villa's rebel army. That was not even close to true. In spite of what he told his followers, El Cuchillo had never actually laid eyes on Pancho Villa let alone served with him.

El Cuchillo, cashing in on the revolutionary fervor, took advantage of the opportunity to raid both countries with impunity, and collecting the benefits of the spoils of war, which sounded much less foul than simple robbery. He appointed himself the rank of Colonel, adding some legitimacy to the crimes of his band.

The bandit and his men traveled between Nogales, Douglas, and sometimes Hermosillo on the Mexican side. They rode as far north as fifty miles into the Estados Unidas carefully avoiding Fort Huachuca and Camp Jones. With only a handful of Arizona Rangers patrolling the border, territorial law enforcement was ill equipped to deal with the invaders. But El Cuchillo had received information from his sources that the American cavalry soldiers had been spoiling for a fight. However, running into a troop of fifty men armed with Springfield Rifles and Benet machine guns was not the odds that El Cuchillo favored for a battle.

El Cuchillo led the rag tag band of criminals down a dirt road in a loose formation. The bandit leader's right hand man, Archuleta, rode up from the rear of the column, taking a position beside El Cuchillo. His face did not conceal his concern about their recent operations. He addressed his leader, as jefe, or boss.

"Jefe," he said quietly so the others would not overhear, "when the Americans find the bodies of those ranchers, there will be hell to pay. They will be up in arms over the death of the child."

49

Archuleta appeared nervous, glancing around the horizon as he spoke.

His words were wasted. El Cuchillo had no patience with anyone second guessing his decisions. He glared with disgust at Archuleta, "We won't be back there for a while. They cannot chase us down here. There is nothing to worry about." El Cuchillo spurred his horse ahead and ended the conversation.

El Cuchillo rode on alone, his men following him southeast out of Nogales and into Mexico. They led a nice string of horses stolen from various ranches in Arizona. The riders were followed by a stolen wagon loaded with booty from their raids. El Cuchillo rode at a walk, at the head of his pack down the dusty Sonoran trail.

The young glory seeker, Jose Lopez next rode up to his leader's side. His agenda differed from Archuleta. He did not share any guilt or concern about their murderous spree. He wanted a favor. "Jefe, the next time we get to Agua Prieta, I would like to cross over and see my mother in Douglas. She prays for my return and I want to take her the jewelry I have for her."

El Cuchillo ignored him. He spurred to a trot, moving away from the boy and headed east, wondering what the boy's mother looked like.

Concern for the needs of his men was not a high priority to the bandit. He could always get more men. Mexico was filled with ignorant peasants who had little value for human life.

Jose flushed with embarrassment, realizing his blathering disturbed the great Colonel and his concentration on the military issues that their small army faced. Jose knew he would have to be more careful in the future, show more respect. Touching the reins, he turned his scrawny mustang and rode back through the dust clouds to the drag position, trailing his fellow outlaws.

# Chapter 4

### Outside of Camp Jones

Private Franky Boothe was a busted luck Texas cowboy who enlisted to avoid unemployment, or worse. It seemed that the ranch owner, who was his prior employer, had a daughter. This daughter had the habit of discussing her paramours quite openly at inopportune times. Unfortunately for Franky, rumors of certain indiscretions seemed to get back to her pa. Franky assumed that his employment was in jeopardy when he saw the cranky old panhandle farmer walk out of the main house over towards the corral having a most disagreeable expression on his face, and toting a double barrel 10 gauge shotgun. Franky heard him say something about castration and since there weren't any colts needing cut, he felt that it might be a good time to take loan of a horse and join the US Army, which he did as quickly as possible.

Fortunately, the Army needed horseman so his quick enlistment went smoothly.

After some training at Jefferson Barracks, he was sent to Fort Huachuca, then to Camp Jones. He had been hoping to be sent to Montana country to see the mountains he had heard so much talk about, but it was just his luck to spend his life picking cactus out of his butt and breathing the dust of the desert just like he had been doing since he was born. To top it all off, he was detailed to drive a wagon load of horse manure to some Mexican lady in Douglas.

All Franky knew of his mission was that Sergeant McGuillicotty had arranged for her garden to receive a substantial amount of government fertilizer in return for fresh vegetables that went to the camp mess. The Mess Sergeant held Top's marker for a card game gone awry and was applying pressure for some kind of payment. As close as Franky could figure, the Mexican lady was sweet on the big mic and was helping him out of his problem. If that was true, Franky was on the bottom of the barrel on this shady deal.

All this wheeling and dealing required too much thinking and that was not in Franky's department. He was slightly better off than being found dead with a belly full of buckshot on a Texas cattle ranch, and was happy to leave it at that.

He whistled and threw some pebbles at the mules to encourage them up a hill. As he took the reins in one hand and wiped his forehead with the other, he thought about his fateful decision to join the Army. Franky hated to admit it but he actually liked the life of a trooper, except for the smell of the shit-wagon detail. Working the nearly two thousand head of cavalry remounts was a cowboy's dream come true. Getting regular food, a regular bunk, and training some pretty decent horseflesh was a lot better than doctoring sick cows and fixing fences in Texas.

He was still learning the ropes of soldiering. He wasn't much of a rifleman yet but he was showing some improvement. He did feel comfortable with his sidearm though. He stroked the model 1911 in his holster. Hell, it just barely 1910 and he had this new-fangled automatic Colt. He laughed out loud as he smacked his team across the ass with his buggy whip and pulled onto Main Street in Douglas. He would damned sure use that Colt on any interlopers wanting to steal his wagon load of horse shit. Yes, the glory of a life in the United States Cavalry, by God, beats the hell out of a West Texas castration any day.

*Daniel Byram*

# Chapter 5

## Naco, Mexico

The Mexican outlaws were just five miles outside of Naco. The band had grown as they travelled, increasing to sixty men. Self-promoted Colonel "*El Cuchillo*" Garcia directed his troops to bed down and care for the horses. The scouts were sent out to try to steal more horses for the valiant revolutionaries who had joined the band on foot. Most of the new soldiers were peons freed by El Cuchillo. Peons, generally indentured servants or people placed into slavery to pay off a debt or for committing a crime, were easy to recruit. They had nothing to lose by joining a revolution and they were already gaining a horse right off the bat. Those who had committed crimes were already considered trained. By delivering them freedom from their obligations, El Cuchillo, in their minds, was a saint and a savior.

The plans were simple: take the small band, steal what horses and supplies that could easily be stolen, and join the other revolutionary forces organizing near Hermosillo. From there, an Army would move to take over the government and perhaps Juan Pedro Garcia would no longer be an outlaw, but become a hero of the revolution and a rich government official. Government meant power, control, and wealth... concepts that appealed to El Cuchillo.

## Stables - Camp Jones

Sergeant McGuillicotty had the daily stable duties completed by noon and was preparing for a restful siesta for the remainder of the day. He felt it was appropriate to conserve his strength after all the effort he put forth in maintaining the honor and reputation of the company the night before.

Bronk had walked to within ten paces of his quarters when Lieutenant Cleary rode up in front of him and stopped in his path. "Sergeant, prepare the men of Troop C and B for a bivouac and training exercise in the San Bernardino Valley. Each man will need two day's rations and 60 rounds of ammunition. My aide, corporal Baxter, will carry my shotgun and 100 rounds of ammunition. We will leave in two hours."

Bronk snapped to attention, "Very good, sir. I will organize the troop. Sergeant Naught on is available and will coordinate for you in the field."

"Perhaps I was unclear, Sergeant," Clearly snarled with barely restrained contempt, "I want *you* to take direct responsibility for this exercise. Please proceed with your duty." Cleary spun his horse and rode out at a lope leaving Bronk sucking dirt.

"Goddamned bloody officer. Can't he see I am not in good enough health for this type of thing. The cursed devil to him," Bronk muttered to himself as he coughed up dust.

Bronk walked over to Corporal Schmidt's tent to give him the order, "Another bloody hunting trip on the Slaughter ranch for that young officer Cleary. Just for once I wish the damn birds would win." He muttered, "I'd like to be the bird to pluck that shave tail."

Bronk threw back the tent flap and squinted into the shadows. "Corporal!" Bronk bellowed rolling misery downhill, "Get your ass over here, and get the troop prepared to move out at once, and be quick about it." Bronk closed the flap, turned, and marched away.

Schmidt scrambled out of the tent after Bronk and began complaining, "We had the afternoon off. What the hell is this all about, Sergeant?"

Bronk was not in the mood for questions. "It's about you doing your damn duty, ya malingering kraut. Now get the troop organized. We move out in an hour, if you don't mind, and be sure each trooper has 100 rounds of ammunition and two day's rations, now move! There will be no more talk of it."

Bronk stomped off toward his tent to pack his medicine and other supplies he would need for field exercises. He grumbled to himself as he walked, "And me in my twilight years, sleeping on the hard, wet ground. It's just not right. Blast that officer's bloody, cold soul." He turned and spit on the ground, and then entered his tent.

The Texas cowboy had returned from his horse manure delivery without incident. He saw to the team and secured the wagon. Trooper Porter ran by and brought him up to date on the maneuvers.

"Get your ass a-rolling son. The Lieutenant is leading a field maneuver and the Top is madder than a stirred up nest of hornets. We all have hell to pay!"

Franky, looking forward to anything but more manure duty, said little. He walked over to his tent and organized his gear. He felt a sense of sadness as he worked, realizing that the days of any *real* action and glory were now over. In this modern army, soldiers just train for the sake of training... preparing for fights that would never happen in the enlightened and modern new century of science and miracles. Franky longed for the glorious days of the big war, the War Between the States, or maybe even the Indian wars... but just riding around the border deterring rustlers was a Marshal's job, not the job of the horse cavalry. He resigned himself to a tedious life and finished packing.

The road from Douglas to San Bernardino Valley stretched sixteen miles along the Mexican border. Its width was sufficient for riding in columns of four.

Lieutenant Cleary led the men down the dusty road, enjoying the obvious discomfort of the foul mouthed, and likely hung over, old Sergeant. Cleary knew he would not have to wait long for McGuillicotty to foul up and provide him with his opportunity to carry out his plan. Then he heard the familiar and annoying thick brogue delivering a blast of profanity... Perfect.

"Private Newton! Get off of that god damned suffering animal and adjust your bloody assed saddle. You folded that Son-of-a-bitching blanket like a..."

Cleary spun his horse and rode between the Sergeant and trooper. "That will be enough Sergeant. You will not address an enlisted man with that language in this Army, Mister. You will consider yourself on report and take a position as the rear guard for the remainder of this assignment!" Cleary spat out the words with disdain.

McGuillicotty stiffened, confused as to what language the lieutenant was referring to. He was busy helping a soldier. But he responded nevertheless with a quick salute and, "Yes, sir."

Cleary looked at the affected trooper and could see Newton's knees begin shaking. "You mister... see to your horse and carry on."

Cleary watched McGuillicotty turn and ride back towards the rear of the column, disappearing into the thick miserable brown dust cloud.

He stopped and cast his gaze over the surrounding men. Cleary noticed they appeared stunned. They must be in awe of me, he thought, impressed with my having the fortitude to face down the brutish McGuillicotty. Cleary was pleased with the result of his intervention and the humiliating dressing down he gave the foul mouthed sergeant. He smiled and resumed his position at the lead of the column.

The road narrowed, forcing the column to ride closer together as the summer heat bore down on them.

Cleary soon became hot and bored. He loped further ahead of the troops. He cleared a slight curve around a small hill when the contraption appeared.

Cleary felt his horse buck and spin out from underneath him, throwing him backwards into the road. He landed hard in the dirt, flat on his back, the wind knocked out of him.

He tried to get up, but his body would not respond to his intent. Frustrated, he closed his eyes and cursed. When he opened them again, he looked up to discover two men standing over him. An old man with a gray whiskbroom beard and a large cigar spoke first, "Boy... boy! Are you alive boy?"

An elderly black man interrupted, "He's alive boss, this soldier is just knocked out! "

A small Chinese man said something that Cleary could not make out, but the other two men nodded in agreement.

The Chinese man and the old-timer helped Cleary to his feet while the black man caught the frightened mount. Cleary felt himself being propped against the fender of some type of motor carriage.

Cleary pushed the men back as they tried to fan him with an old dirty handkerchief, ineffectively trying to restore his dignity and distance himself from the dusty interlopers. He groaned with embarrassment as he saw the troops arrive and discover his predicament

Sergeant McGuillicotty rode up to the motor carriage and dismounted. "Top of the day to you Mr. Slaughter, " he addressed the old man with his thick brogue.

"I think I almost killed one of your men here with my motor carriage Sergeant Bronk," Slaughter explained sheepishly.

Cleary interrupted the old man and emphatically attempted to clarify his role in the military procession, "*I*, my good man, am *not* one of *this* individual's men. *I*," he paused for effect, "am in *command* of this detail."

Slaughter stared at him without moving for a few seconds and then snorted, "Isn't it hard to command these soldiers while you're laying in the road, boy? "

Cleary regrouped his thoughts, straightening his blouse and then queried the old man, "Your name, sir? "

"John Slaughter, the former Sheriff of these parts. I imagine it's my ranch you're riding on, sonny. Now what in the name of heaven is *your* name, boy?"

Cleary slumped, recognizing that he was engaging in pointless bickering with one of the most influential men in the territory. He came to

attention. "Lieutenant Cleary, sir... at your service."
Cleary served at Camp Jones long enough to be
fully aware of the strategic importance of Mr.
Slaughter's ranch, beef, and hospitality to the US
Army. "Mr. Slaughter, if you will please excuse us,
we shall continue with our assignment."

The black man returned with Cleary's horse,
handed him the reins, and the Lieutenant
mounted.

Cleary looked ahead and gave the command to
move out. "Good day, sir."

Slaughter climbed back into his motor carriage.
He spoke to the black man who was driving, "Old
Bat, I think that boy is a little high strung for these
parts, don't you believe?"

Bat responded with a nod, "I surely hope Mr.
Bronk can teach him how to ride a horse."

Slaughter, who rarely smiled, laughed out loud
at his trusted friend's comment. "Well, let's get Joe
Lee into town so he can get his supplies. We'll
leave the soldiering to Mister Bronk."

# Chapter 6

## Sonora, Mexico: Near the Rurale Headquarters

Miguel Suarez was not a happy man. As one of the Mexican 'Rurales' border militia, he was stationed at a remote border station about eighteen miles east of Agua Prieta. His duty was to guard the border, but to guard it from what, he was not sure. He suspected that he was there to watch out for those damned gringo outlaws and all the trouble they bring. The rustlers still frequently cross into Mexico and steal livestock or sell stolen livestock for a living, but more and more of them were involved in smuggling supplies to the criminal revolutionaries who were tearing apart the great country of Mexico.

The members of the Rurale border guards usually consisted of peasants and misfits. Miguel was the former. The militia groups typically financed their operations by extorting funds from travelers, which in Miguel's mind, sounded a lot like stealing. He was not raised that way, but... he was a proud defender of Mexico, even if it was done somewhat shamefully.

Miguel dreamed of serving Mexico in the Army of Diaz, as a warrior defending his country, instead of serving as a Rurale border guard with those other fat lazy pigs who wanted nothing to do with real work. El teniente Moreno, the lieutenant in charge of their detail, was an arrogant martinet and coward. The teniente did not give a damn in regard for Miguel because Miguel did not spend his day feeding the teniente's inflated ego like the other sycophants at their post. Miguel was an 'hombre, a real man... he needed adventure. He dreamed of glory.

While Miguel pondered the cruelty of his fate, the change of luck he prayed for slowly wandered into his patrol area. Breaking through the brush were two gringo soldiers. They did not see Miguel. The soldiers were concentrating on locating a pheasant.

## Chapter 7

### Near the border

On the last eight or so miles of the seventeen mile trip from Camp Jones, McGuillicotty suffered the error of his ways from the night before. "Mother Mary, full of grace, I'm through with drinking forever, this time I mean it, amen" he mumbled his oft abused prayer. His head throbbed and the unsettled condition of his stomach required that he make numerous humbling trips to the bushes.

When they finally arrived at the campsite, he organized the weary troopers into their assignments and directed the set up of the camp. He began to feel a little better having a chance to get out of the saddle and walk around in the cool San Bernardino Valley air, off the dusty road. He looked around for his Officer to find if there was to be further orders and noticed Cleary was gone.

"The damned Lieutenant has already gone off bird hunting with his bloody dog robber Baxter," he growled with significant disgust in his tone.

For troop morale, McGuillicotty knew he could not allow the men know that the true purpose of this training exercise was to create a sporting opportunity for an arrogant officer to go off

69

pheasant hunting. He grabbed the senior corporal by the sleeve and gave him an assignment.

"Corporal Schmidt, please see to the mounts, be quick with ya. Make sure these new recruits have properly watered and secured them, and when you finish with that then prepare the men for chow. I'll be checking in with the Lieutenant in the field to see if he needs assistance in scouting the 'exercise' we are planning tomorrow," he said, reluctantly covering for the hoax mission.

Bronk lit a cigar and enjoyed a long drag. He exhaled deeply, then began chewing nervously on the butt. He sensed something was wrong, but couldn't quite figure out what it was, maybe it was just the hangover.

Schmidt watched Bronk's attempt at being inconspicuous as the big sergeant strolled over to his horse and prepared to ride out of camp. Everyone in the troop knew what was going on. Bronk was fooling no one. Schmidt couldn't understand for the life of him, one good reason for Sergeant Bronk to cover for that worthless pimple on a good Lieutenant's ass. Why didn't Bronk come straight out and just admit that this training maneuver fiasco was just an excuse for the Lieutenant's hunting trip? Well, what goes on inside the big mic's head was beyond Schmidt's imagination. It was no secret, that was for sure. The Lieutenant knew it, Bronk knew it, and the men knew it. Lieutenant Cleary and that knot headed Baxter were out shooting birds and wasting the very valuable time of good soldiers. What confused Schmidt the most was, he knew Top had no use for the arrogant, young, and foolish Lieutenant. It just didn't make sense. He didn't like it.

McGuillicotty saddled Mac and rode out of camp without a further word to anyone. He headed south, looking for the errant officer and aide, just to ease his mind.

He rode for what seemed to him like a hell of a long ways, far closer to the border than they should be, and yet he still saw no sign of them. Bronk continued another ten minutes south. He came down into a wash and finally located their mounts tethered on the Mexican side of the line. Very bad... Their tracks indicated that they continued even further south from there. Bronk wished he had Big Ugly with him.

"Well Mac, here we are again, on the wrong side of the border." Bronk still harbored some grudges against the country of Mexico from the night before, the dirty fighters. He took a drink from his canteen and swirled it around in his mouth. He spit it out and attached the canteen back to his McClellan. He thought about it for a moment and considered that maybe the country of Mexico might be holding a few grudges against him too.

Bronk sought the counsel of his trusted horse, "Mac, me boy, where do you think our fine young officer wandered off to down here in this god forsaken country of dirty fighters and drunkards? " Bronk stroked the Morgan's thick neck with a gloved hand. The big horse softly nickered.

Bronk stopped stroking Mac and frowned at him, "No Mac, I just can't leave him here and take the bloody horses back. That goes against the oath of a sergeant, it does, and I'm ashamed of ya for even suggesting it."

Mac answered by raising his tail and depositing road apples on the desert floor.

Smiling, Bronk leaned forward and fondly scratched his horse behind the ears, "You're not the first soldier to suggest I might be full of it."

A slight wiggle in the McClellan saddle was Mac's cue to walk out. Bronk quietly circled the area in a rough search pattern, occasionally glassing the brushy desert with his field binoculars. He forced himself not to laugh out loud when he saw a young Mexican soldier about 250 yards east of his location marching Cleary and Baxter off as prisoners... and using the Lieutenants own model 97 Winchester shotgun holding them at gunpoint.

Bronk whispered to Mac, " Did ya see that me boy, he's even making Baxter carry a dead pheasant."

Mac turned his head back rolling a big black eye towards his rider in acknowledgment.

"Aye, it looks like those Mexican lads might be having that fine bird for dinner, compliments of our own officer and gentleman, the famous Lieutenant Cleary, recently graduated from West Point."

From what Bronk could make out in the field glasses, the young soldier looked to be a border guard. Bronk recalled that they were known as Rurales in Mexico, and they were generally focused on the business of extorting money from travelers, rather than securing the frontier. They were not to be mistaken for Mexican Army regulars, more like organized outlaws with some sort of nod of approval from the local government.

"Duty comes before pleasure, Mac," the Sergeant restrained his laughter at the cocky lieutenant's plight. Bronk quietly shadowed the trio to the Rurale headquarters about a mile and a half further south of the border. From his position, he counted half a dozen armed Mexican militia gathering around as the young soldier brought his prisoners into the camp. The camp consisted of a stone building and a couple of adobe outbuildings with some tents and shades set up.

Bronk strained to listen, but was too far away to hear what was being said. He could see Cleary physically protesting his capture. Bronk watched as Cleary jerked his arm away from the boy who captured him and shake his finger in the face of a fat soldier who was wearing a red sash. The fat man did not like it. He quickly drew his pistol and struck the Lieutenant solidly on the side of the head, dropping him to his knees, blood running down his face.

Bronk's jaw tightened and his hand instinctively went to his rifle scabbard. He caught himself before he pulled his rifle, stopping to consider appropriate military tactics.

"Mac, me boy, we might be able to take on the garrison alone in a fair fight, but the chances are good that the Lieutenant and Corporal will get themselves killed by these blasted Rurales in the process... damn it... that would annoy the Colonel."

Mac snorted in agreement.

Bronk got up and gently nudged Mac's flank with a knee, wheeling the big horse around and walking out of hearing range of the border station. Then he sank spurs, making best time back to his own camp.

At the Rurale headquarters, Lieutenant Moreno expressed his shock and dismay at the initiative taken by young Suarez. He never had anyone in his command ever do anything before that would force him to make a decision. Life had been simple, rob the gringo, rob the Mexican, whoever crossed the border with money or property, give his fair share to the Rurales, like it or not. But now they had American soldiers in custody. This is much more complicated. Moreno had become a leader in the Rurales based on his ruthlessness, not brain.

He stared at the ground looking over the injured American, realizing that *now* he has an unconscious gringo officer and a gringo soldier in his custody. He asked himself, 'How will I ever explain after this?

He bellowed accusingly, "Suarez, you stupid bastard. What he hell do you think you are doing? This is a goddamned gringo officer! " He jabbed the bleeding Cleary, accenting each syllable with a poke of his finger.

Sergeant Delgado spoke up, trying to be a voice of reason, adjusted the red sash holding his fat belly and pistol, "Jefe, I think these two pendejos are just a scouting party of spies sent by the Americans to survey our strength. I recommend we take them over to the wash to the west of the building a kill them both. They will probably never be missed."

"No Sergeant, these men probably will be *missed*," Moreno smiled, "but I don't think they will ever be found."

Suarez looked about as his fellow peasant soldiers gathered, all conscripts, mostly poor local farmers, nervously clustering around the Americans. It was obvious to Suarez that the other men were frightened too, and all thinking the same thing. None of them wanted to be involved with killing these gringos in cold blood. These soldiers did not appear to be spies or invaders. They were most likely to be part of a unit that was lost. Would it be murder to kill them?

Murder was not what Suarez had in mind when he captured the men. He expected they would be questioned and then eventually returned to their post. The men of the little Rurale outpost would all have something to talk about for a while. After seeing the cruel Delgado hit the gringo officer with the pistol, that would not be the case. Killing these soldiers might be a mistake. Killing these soldiers might be the death of them all.

Moreno looked over to Delgado with disgust, "The damage is done, Sergeant. When we are finished questioning these men, kill them, and bury them deep. Then bring me their guns and money. Then when you have finished doing that, beat the hell out of that idiot Suarez for causing these problems."

Suarez knew what fate Moreno's plan would bring to the little outpost. The men did not come here for this. They came because they were eager for opportunities to do their duty, to have glorious stories to take back to their small towns someday. Although they were uneducated and simple peons, they all knew that killing these Americans would be an act of cold blooded murder. What would they do when other American soldiers came looking for them? They all knew the answer to that question. American reprisals would be swift and sure, and they will all be killed. Nobody was going to go home.

Skidding from a blistering gallop to a dead stop, Mac sank his butt down and slid into the encampment as Bronk made a flying dismount. "Corporal Schmidt! Corporal Blue! Damn it boys, get the troops mounted and issue the extra ammunition. The bloody Rurales have taken the Lieutenant and Baxter prisoner! Hurry boys!"

The usually understated Schmidt jumped up, threw down his plate of beans, and raced over to the dust cloud created by Mac's stop. "Are you sure they can't just keep him a while Top?" He was still uncertain as to whether or not this was another McGuillicotty prank. The look on Bronk's face told him something different.

"Damn it man, me thinks they will kill him and damned quick. Form up two squads and have the squad leaders meet me here. Be quick about it."

The Sergeant and Corporals hunkered in a semi-circle around Bronk. He kneeled down and drew a map in the dirt with his knife. "I'll take Private Boothe and move right in under their blasted noses on the East side. Blue, Give me twenty minutes lead, and then have Bruner give the bugle call for a charge. I want one squad of the boys to come in from the North and one from the West. We can converge on the bastards and push them south once we have our men out. Now listen carefully boys, these murdering bastards will try to kill the Lieutenant as soon as trouble starts. If I can get me big arse into the door first, we will take Baxter and Cleary away from them." He drew a line with the knife tip. "Then we push all the rest of the bastards who are still alive south and then disengage. All we want is to get our bloody officer and soldier back. But make no mistake boys, any son of bitch who kills a US soldier is damned well going to die for their mistake." He looked into the face of each man and said solemnly, "We are the only hope these men have. Questions?"

None of the men responded, but Bronk could see the answer in their faces. The mission was clear. Their fellow soldiers were facing certain death and no true American would let that happen without doing everything possible to save them.

Bronk wiped the knife on his pants and put it back in the sheath.

"Then see to your troops boys." The big man stood and walked briskly to his horse and began organizing his equipment for battle.

The troops were briefed by their squad leaders, then nervously prepared for action. McClellans were cinched tight... ammunition and weapons were checked and rechecked.

The daydreams of glory in battle from earlier in the day quickly vanished. Franky Boothe had an overpowering urge to piss his pants. Lord God Almighty, he was going to war... a shooting war. And he was riding with the craziest sumbitch in the horse cavalry, Sergeant Bronk Mcguillicotty. Franky's thoughts raced as he prepared his equipment. *I sure didn't want to die in Mexico. Dang bad luck. I guess I should have stayed in Texas where my dumb ass belongs.*

He saw Bronk walking toward him, a grim look on his face. Franky noticed the little dust clouds that sprang from the dry desert floor at each step of the Sergeant's cavalry boots. He could not control his shaking knees, and hoped Bronk didn't notice. He looked up at six foot-four inches of fighting man, a man who stopped about an inch away from Franky's nose. The voice was a whisper, "Laddie, I picked you because you're a good Texas man. I never knew a Texan who was bothered by fighting. Almost all of them I ever knew like it. Stay close with me and when the time comes, I want you to fight like hell. You will know what to do. I know you will."

Franky's jaw dropped as the behemoth strode off to his horse. He asked himself, "The meanest son of a bitch I ever knew is asking for me to stand with him in a fight?" He took a plug of chaw and jumped up on the back of his mount. "Damned right I'll know what to do."

*Daniel Byram*

## Chapter 8

Sitting in an uncomfortable crouch on a small milking stool, Cleary felt like his head was going to snap off at the neck as Delgado and Moreno stood over him taking turns slapping him, delivering powerful strikes against the side of the head followed by cruel backhands. The tormentors laughed as they tried to outdo each other, seeing how much pain they could inflict. The sadists were enjoying it too much. He forced a swollen eye open and saw Baxter laying on the floor with his hands tied behind his back. He winced as the fat Delgado smashed his face with a closed fist almost knocking him off the crude seat.

Cleary spoke, "For God's sake, what do you want? "

"This gringo wants to know what we want, jefe... What do we want?" Delgado asked laughing.

Moreno answered Cleary directly, "Nada, Teniente. We don't want a damned thing."

Both Rurales roared with laughter. Delgado slapped Cleary against the back of the head knocking him face first into the floor.

The other Mexican soldiers waited near the desert wash outside the building. They were desperately trying to figure out a way to avoid participating in the murder of the Americans.

They had little hope the gringo soldados would live through the brutal questioning by their sadistic commanders. But the blood would still be on their hands, at least in the vengeful eyes of the United States Army.

Suarez addressed his fellow peasant soldiers, "We can't murder these men. It isn't right."

Another soldier responded cautiously, "I don't think we have to kill them. I think all we will have to do is bury them."

"Yes, "said another, "And the rest of the Americans will kill us all just the same... but leave our bones for the coyotes and buzzards."

Cleary held his own during the beating, "I am an officer in the United States Army. I was merely traveling to Texas with my aide when we became lost. You are going to release us with escort back to the border or there will be hell to pay!"

Cleary was answered by a smashing fist against the side of his head that split the skin above his left eye. Moreno laughed, "Of course, Teniente, just as soon as we finish your lesson in courtesy to the government of Mexico."

Baxter tried to speak out, but was muffled with

a solid kick to the face by Delgado. He collapsed limply to a fetal position, blood pouring from his nose and mouth.

Cleary's hands were bound in front of him with a piece of rawhide. Although severely stunned by the beating, he was still rational enough to evaluate his situation. He knew that by now he was overdue at the camp. He had to assume that McGuillicotty would take charge and send a courier back to Camp Jones for orders. He also figured he would be dead by the time a decision was made. His aide was unconscious and would be of no help. Cleary accepted the fact that if he was going to live, he was going to have to deal with the Mexicans himself. His hand slowly slipped down by his boot.

McGuillicotty and Boothe squatted behind cover to the east of the small building where the Lieutenant was being held. They had about forty yards of open ground, extending from the desert brush they concealed themselves in, to the front door of the building. Boothe felt his knees shaking again. He looked to McGuillicotty's face, but it appeared as though it was chiseled from stone. Bronk's blank expression appeared more like a man concentrating on reading a newspaper rather than a soldier planning a suicidal dash for the door of the Rurales' headquarters.

McGuillicotty placed his hand on Boothe's shoulder and whispered, "Steady boy. Don't think about getting killed or you will certainly die. Just think about killing those bastards first and you'll be fine."

Boothe made a confession, "Sergeant, I'm scared shitless."

Bronk stiffened, "Well do you think the Lieutenant *isn't*, goddamn it? If it was your sorry ass in that building lad, we'd damned sure be doing the same for you. You are part of our company. The Lieutenant is part of our company. It's what the horse cavalry is all about. Son, you can be scared as you want, but by God, do your duty. The Lieutenant is counting on you." Bronk glowered at the young trooper for a second, then added, "You'll be fine. Just stay with me." With that, the talking ended and Bronk refocused his attention on the job at hand.

Across the clearing at the wash, Schmidt could see the horses were starting to sense the nervousness of their riders. The mounts slobbered at their bits. Lather was building up on the flanks around the McClellans. The younger horses were prancing. Schmidt looked at his watch and then nodded at the squad leaders. He then gave the command, "Weapons at the ready." The men drew pistols The Springfield rifles were left in their scabbards. They all knew fight would be close and dirty. Corporal Schmidt took another look at his pocket watch, then drew his saber and whispered loud enough for the troops to hear, "At the trot... forward."

Bronk held a bayonet in his right hand and his pistol in the left. The expression of concentration he bore had turned into a mask of hatred. He growled under his breath, "By God, let's do it boys."

Schmidt called over his right shoulder to Bruner, "At the command, blow that damned bugle, Bruner " He shouted to the squad, "At the gallop - *Charge!*"

The bugle pierced the evening air. Spurs sank into horseflesh. Men and horses burst through the brush and into the clearing. Schmidt's squad came up the dry wash at a dead run, nearly trampling the Rurale sentries who broke and ran in confusion. The cavalry mounts crashed into fleeing

Mexican soldiers knocking them to the ground. The troopers didn't slow down to take prisoners and continued a maniacal charge toward the Rurale headquarters.

On foot, Bronk rushed from cover at a sprint with Boothe at his side, not slowing when he hit the wooden door with his massive bulk. The door splintered, and Bronk rolled into the center of the room before he heard Bruner finish sounding the charge on his bugle.

When the door exploded apart from the force of McGuillicotty's shoulder, Cleary used the confusion to reach into his boot pulling out a small dagger. With his hands still bound at the wrist in front of him, Cleary jammed the six inch blade to the hilt directly above Moreno's groin, then twisted the blade left and right. He could feel the warm blood from Moreno's abdomen running down his arm.

Moreno's face contorted with the shock of the wound but was stunned for only a moment. He began clubbing the Cleary in the face with his pistol. Screaming curses in Spanish he tried to finish Cleary, but Cleary didn't quit. Moreno's eyes widened in horror as the Lieutenant rose to his knees driving the knife farther, tearing deeper into

Moreno's bleeding guts.

Across the room Bronk smashed his shoulder into Delgado's chest, knocking him to the ground stunned and disoriented. McGuillicotty fell clumsily on the fat tormentor, jamming the bayonet with all of his strength deep in Delgado's bowels . Delgado tried to scream, but instead gagged as Bronk jammed his pistol barrel in the fat man's mouth and pulled the trigger. The report in the little room was deafening. The top of Delgado's head exploded spraying the fighters with a red mist.

Boothe crashed across the doorway and immediately fell over the prone figure of Baxter. He looked up in shock as Moreno clubbed Cleary repeatedly across the face with his pistol. Booth saw Cleary pushing up with the dagger, opening the midsection of Moreno. Even as guts rolled out on the floor, Moreno continued beating the American officer. From the floor, Boothe took a quick shot at Delgado's head and missed. He rose to his feet and placed the muzzle against Delgado's temple and pulled the trigger. The .45 caliber pistol round achieved a muzzle velocity of 810 feet per second when it hit the side of Moreno's skull. The slow moving round penetrated his head deeply but didn't exit. All the back pressure was blown out the entrance wound causing a spray of brains and bone to strike Boothe square in the face, pushing the bloody matter in his mouth, nose and eyes. Boothe fell back in shock believing he had been killed, and lost control of his bladder.

Moreno lurched to the side and fell with a badly injured Cleary rolling over on top of him.

Cleary could see Moreno was dead, but in a fit of rage, he still slowly cut his throat, nearly decapitating his tormentor.

Bronk got to his feet and quickly cleared the rest of the building find no one else inside. He checked Baxter for signs of life. He found a pulse, Baxter was alive but barely conscious and bleeding from the head profusely.

Cleary blinked the blood out of one eye. He took a breath... the rage subsided... he regained his sanity, not really believing he just killed a man. He had never even been in a fight before. And now he brutally murdered a man with a knife.

No one said a word...

Cleary recovered his senses and spoke first, his voice almost inaudible, "Sergeant McGuillicotty, would you be so kind as to untie my hands? "

Bronk turned, pulled the knife out of Moreno's neck and cut through the rawhide cord, "Will there be anything else then, sir? " He gently helped the officer to his feet and returned the dagger.

Cleary, standing on unstable legs, tried to straighten his clothes, "Please see to my aide, Sergeant."

"Yes sir," McGuillicotty replied.

Cleary started to regain his composure in spite of his horribly wounded face. Without passionate or other emotion, he continued with clipped syntax, "Then, assemble the men and let's get the hell out of here." He punctuated his order by spitting a mouthful of blood on his disemboweled torturer. Maybe the rage wasn't all gone yet.

Mcguillicotty ignored the expectoration and gave only a curt nod. He answered, "Very good, sir."

As the remainder of the troop waited outside surrounding the building, Schmidt and Blue entered with pistols drawn, unsure who the victors were going to be from the fight. Bronk heard the noise and spun with his pistol and Cleary pointed the dagger towards the door. They recognized the intruders as their fellow soldiers immediately and lowered their weapons. Blue looked over the carnage, "Jesus, Joseph, and Mary ." He subconsciously crossed himself and walked back out, "Troops, take any stragglers as prisoner and form up in front of this building.

Within five minutes, the men were assembled in the front of the building with the rurale survivors, most of whom simply surrendered at the first opportunity, waiting for the Corporal to return with orders. Blue and Schmidt came out first carrying the unconscious Baxter. Even the most experienced troopers stared in disbelief when Bronk and Boothe, with Cleary supported between them, came out. Three figures, covered with blood, gore, and brain matter. Cleary stopped and looked over the troops. He paused for a moment, then spoke, "Gentlemen, I thank you for this valiant rescue. These two soldiers and I..." Cleary stopped and grimaced as agonizing pain overcame him. He took a deep breath and gathered himself, "We must see to our deportment. Please organize the prisoners into a burial detail for their commanders, then prepare to move out for camp." Cleary turned his head towards the cabin and smiled, "I had a nice pheasant in there somewhere that would make a decent addition to dinner for us, if one of you would be so kind as to fetch it for me."

The three men then limped to the well and began the painful process of cleaning wounds and wiping off the red stains of close quarters battle.

Boothe was still visibly disturbed, "Sergeant, I

can't stop shaking, and I think I pissed my pants."

"Don't worry Franky my boy, I would have pissed mine too, but I just didn't have to go. You did real good son. You did fine. I'm proud of you."

Franky Boothe had never had anyone be proud of him before. The display of confidence by his Sergeant caused his eyes to tear. He turned his head so Bronk wouldn't see. He stopped as the reality of the situation overcame him, "Sarge, we killed those men in there. It was murder. Jesus Christ."

"Aye Franky, we damned sure did. And if we had not killed them, they were going to kill our man for sure. It's just part of soldiering, son. You did what you had to do. A soldier's work."

Lieutenant Cleary was holding a damp cloth to the side of his face and using another one to wipe the blood off his clothing. "Sergeant, those men were about to murder us." He looked Bronk in the eye. "You came not a moment too soon."

"We came as fast as we could, sir."

"I'm not going to forget this Sergeant McGuillicotty. You could have left us, sent a dispatcher, and awaited orders. That is standard procedure. You could have done that."

"Not in this company, sir. Not with our soldiers."

### Camp Jones

At noon the next day, the pickets rushed in with the word of the skirmish. Colonel Mason hurried out to the parade ground to see the worst looking excuse for a living human he had seen in some time leading the detail.

Lieutenant Cleary stopped in front of the Colonel and saluted. "The troop has engaged a hostile force, sir. May I give my report." Cleary swayed in the saddle.

"Keep it brief Lieutenant, you look as if you're dying on me."

"I *have* felt better, sir."

Cleary abruptly fell off his horse, landing in a heap on the ground.

Colonel Mason did not flinch. He remained at parade rest. "Men, get the lieutenant to the surgeon's tent." He stated the order matter of factly, as though he was telling a child to pick up his toys. "Sergeant McGuillicotty, please meet me in my quarters for the report." Mason stood fast while the men got Cleary to his feet and carried him away.

Mason sat behind the simple table that served as his desk. Bronk stood at attention on front of it. Mason addressed Bronk curtly, "Does this camp need to prepare for a defensive action, Sergeant?"

"No sir. I do not believe we will have any incursions onto American soil. The prisoners tell me that the Mexican government had forgotten about them anyway and..."

"PRISONERS! What prisoners? You cannot invade a sovereign foreign government on the authority of a Second Lieutenant, abduct citizens out of there, and bring them into the United States. Have you lost your mind? " Mason's eyes bulged and a vein in his forehead looked as though it might burst.

"I'm sorry, sir. The raid was actually initiated on my authority," McGuillicotty turned his nose up and sniffed.

Colonel Mason sank back into his chair. He directed a vacant gaze toward his portrait of Theodore Roosevelt in a vain act of seeking guidance. "A Sergeant authorized an invasion of Mexico. Heaven forgive us," he confessed to Teddy's stern countenance.

McGuillicotty continued, "Well, there is a little more to it than that sir, if I may explain."

Mason shook his head in disbelief, "Make it good Sergeant McGuillicotty, all our asses are on the line on this one."

McGuillicotty made it good. He gave a detailed

report in an orderly and efficient military manner. Mason did not know if it was good enough for headquarters, but it was good enough for him.

When he finished his report, the Sergeant came to attention, holding a salute in an effort to reinforce the veracity of his statement.

Mason absorbed what he heard for a moment, then leaned back in his chair and lit a cigar. "Not exactly by the book, McGuillicotty... But... I can't say I wouldn't have done the same thing. Sergeant, See to your men... and secure the, uh...*prisoners*. If the lieutenant is well enough, have him join me for dinner this evening. You're dismissed."

Bronk saluted.

Mason stood at attention and returned a salute to the grizzled Sergeant.

Bronk spun around and marched to the door. Mason sat back down in his chair. He spoke again before the sergeant left, "Bronk, one more thing. Is Cleary going to work out all right?"

Bronk turned and faced his commander, "He'll do just fine, Colonel Darling, just fine indeed." Bronk paused, and then added, "I suspect he will be having the soup this evening though, sir."

# Chapter 9

## Camp Jones - October 12, 1911

Trooper Boothe heard the stable call and started towards the main coral. With slight knee pressure, he turned the Morgan gelding and gave him his head. Two hundred remounts were in the herd he was bringing in off the grassy range four miles to the east of the camp. The herd kicked up a dust cloud so thick that visibility was limited to about eight feet and the noise was as thunderous as a Texas tornado. Boothe reined with his left hand and shook his rope at the horse next to him with his right. A sharp whistle and a, "*Yaahh*" did not make them move any faster. The herd was cavalry remounts. The horses knew the bugle calls too and would have stampeded for the corrals whether Franky was there or not. Still, the ride was exhilarating. Franky sucked in dirt with mouth open in a big grin.

The Texas cowboy was in his height of glory. The new gelding he was working was probably the best horse he had ever rode. He loved the cavalry life. It was a hard life and for many men, a short one. But for the first time in his life, Boothe felt like he had a family. He knew he had a home in the horse cavalry.

With the herd secured in the West corrals, Boothe stepped down off the Morgan and tethered him to the corral with his neck rope. Boothe heard it before he saw it. Some type of disturbance had broken out in camp. Nearly fifty men were enveloped in a dust cloud that had been kicked up on the East end of the corral area. From the cursing and cheering, Boothe suspected a soldiers' fight. He moved in the direction of the melee quickly.

A gigantic ham hock came off the ground, impacted a big round human head, and launched it up into the air. The body followed the general trajectory of the head, and the entire mass landed in a heap in the dust. The body behind the fist jumped into the air in an attempt to smash the other fighter into the earth with a massive belly smacker. McGuillicotty rolled and Sergeant Major Elmer Young landed face first in the dirt. His great belly broke the jarring impact of the crash. McGuillicotty drew back a grand Irish-Polish fist of his own and prepared for a skull bashing right to Young's nose.

One of Young's buffalo soldiers reached in and grabbed McGuillicotty's hand, preventing him from throwing a punch, with the intention of helping out his Sergeant Major. This misguided act of kindness only enraged Elmer Young more. If there was one thing he hated, it was someone interfering in his personal affairs. Young scrambled to his feet and dropped a left cross bomb into the side of the buffalo soldier's head, knocking him immediately unconscious... and knocking two other nearby bystanders off their feet.

Franky Boothe was nearing the scene of the excitement when a concealed spectator grabbed him by the arm. "Don't waste your time placing a bet son, these always end up a draw." The observer moved back into the shadows, grinning from ear to ear.

Franky was more stunned by the covert advice of Colonel Mason than he was by the sight of Bronk McGuillicotty and the huge black sergeant duking it out in the horse shit.

Both combatants were on their feet and circling, each with a headlock on the other. They grunted and cursed... neither had a clear advantage.

Boothe saw his pal Blue in the crowd and moved near him for a closer look. Corporal Blue put his arm around Boothe. "Isn't this a grand time Boothe, old son? This is the third one I have seen since I've been here. Every time the Tenth comes out, this happens. It's like a tradition." Blue flinched dramatically as Pappy punched Bronk below the belt, "Damn, that had to hurt." He redirected his attention back to Boothe, "It starts with an arm wrestling match between Bronk and old Pappy, and ends up with an old fashioned donnybrook. Pretty soon an officer will come out and break it up."

"Hell, won't they go to the guard house for this? " Boothe spoke out the side of his mouth as his eyes were riveted on the fighters.

"Heavens no, boy. The colonel needs both of them on duty to keep the rest of us from finding trouble this evening."

"Won't they get to fighting again? I figured you'd have to kill Bronk onced you commenced to trying to whip him."

Blue looked at Boothe as though he had caught him defecating upstream from camp. "Now why would they fight again? They're best friends... they served in Cuba together."

Both soldiers turned in time to see Lieutenant Cleary, the Corporal of the Guard, and ten men who were volunteered for guard duty, break through the crowd. They pull the two filthy hulks apart.

The men stopped fighting but still put up some

mild resistance.

Clearly spoke, "Gentlemen, and I use the term quite loosely in the context of this situation, please report the circumstances of this display of roughnecking." Cleary arrogantly stood with his shoulders back and nose in the air as only he could do it.

Bronk started, "Beggin' the Lieutenant's pardon sir, but me-self and Sergeant Major Young was just telling the boys about the battle of San Juan Hill and how we found ourselves fighting for our bloody lives against the Spaniards, sir... Outnumbered we were, one hundred to one. And of course not a cursed bullet between us."

The black man interrupted in his heavy southern accent, "That's right, suh. That hand to hand fighting was all we had between us and certain death, suh. We wuz just showin' the boys. Helping them to be ready. Training, suh, yes suh, training. That's what Sergeant McGuillicotty was explaining, suh."

McGuillicotty butted in, "That's right sir, and if it wasn't for our own beloved Sergeant teaching us as lads, we would not have been the lone survivors of that engagement with himself, Colonel Roosevelt, at our side."

Cleary had about all of the thick Irish brogue

and Alabama southern drawl as he wanted to hear for one afternoon. "Both of you report to your quarters, clean up, and excuse yourselves from the post for the remainder of the day. Gentlemen, you're dismissed." Cleary snapped to attention, turned about face, and made it to his tent before he burst into laughter.

Back in the corral, Young whispered to his opponent, "Do you think he believed it, Bronk? " Pappy Young was still standing rigidly at attention.

Bronk, also standing at attention, nodded enthusiastically, "Oh, absolutely Pappy. How can he help but believe the word of a man with me reputation for the truth above all other things. Besides that, the boy looks up to me as a sort of father figure, you know. Now let's get into to town and I'll buy you a tequila."

"I've always wanted to try it. I hear it's very good."

"Me too, I've heard the same thing... after you, Sergeant."

"Thank you, Sergeant."

The two marched off to the stables to clean up, their heads held high as if leading a parade.

The next day was not going to be easy. The men of the Tenth brought over new recruits from

Fort Huachuca for basic horsemanship training. The Sergeants and Corporals organized their classes in groups of eight. The large supply of remounts and the new jumping training course made Camp Jones the perfect location to start out the green riders.

The first day of training consisted of familiarization with the equipment and saddling. Some of the cowboys who joined up were more used to the Mexican saddles that were so common in the area. The high cantle and pommel with the large saddle horn found on the heavy local saddles was quite a bit different from the lightweight McClellan that had served the Army for so many years.

Corporal Blue and Private Boothe were assigned to teach a class on folding the blanket and saddling the horse. Boothe went through the nomenclature of the saddle, and Blue began to demonstrate the proper way to fold the Army blanket.

A salty cowboy from Prescott started to argue with them, "I been on horses for my whole life and I don't need somebody telling me how to fold up a damned blanket."

"Well, I suspect you better never allow your horse to get a sore back then, or the sergeant will take it out of your danged hide."

"What the hell do I care if that nag gets a sore back, these horses are for using, not some dandified, funny-saddled parade!"

Blue's face turned red as he clenched a fist and started to step forward. Boothe put a hand on his shoulder and softly cleared his throat.

Blue stopped long enough to see that Sergeant Bronk McGuillicotty and Sergeant Elmer Young had stepped out of nowhere and were standing directly behind the mouthy cowboy.

The cowboy continued his tirade. "I joined up to ride, not to get escorted around by a bunch of colored boys and taught how to ride on that stupid looking sissy saddle."

As the last words exited his mouth, the cowboy launched forward like a cannon shot and landed on his face in the dirt. The other recruits stepped back quickly lest McGuillicotty land his big foot in the seat of their pants too.

Bronk lifted the cowboy to his feet by his ear, "We prefer to call our comrades, Buffalo Soldiers, or just soldiers, or comrades in arms, not colored boys."

Pappy Young grabbed the other ear and raised the cowboy to his tiptoes, "If we're in the field and that horse gives out on you because you didn't take care of it properly, then you're of no use to me. In this outfit, if you are of no use, we have to waste a bullet on you to put you down, and I surely don't like to waste the army's bullets. Is that clear enuf, private? "

The cowboy nodded briskly rubbing the seat of his breaches, "Yes, Sergeants."

McGuillicotty cut in, "Then maybe you better tell us you respect your horse."

"Yes, Sergeant, I respect my horse, " the cowboy winced as he answered in a high pitched voice.

The Sergeants let go of his ears and gave him a nudge back into the group of recruits. "If there be no further questions, lads, please go back to your class, and remember, six layers thick on the blanket."

Blue and Boothe forced themselves not to smile and continued the training session uninterrupted.

Franky and Blue sat on the back end of an old wagon near the boundaries of the camp and watched the beautiful show of color than is an Arizona sunset as they shared a small flask of whiskey. Miguel Suarez approached them, walking from the stables having just finished his duties as a somewhat unclassified prisoner of an undeclared war.

"Miguel, what did you find out? " Blue asked in barely passable Spanish as he handed him the flask.

"Nada, amigo. It is my wish to stay, but there is talk we may be going home next week, " Miguel responded in English. He took a sip of whiskey and handed the flask back.

"Hell compadre, you been here nine months now. I ain't sure, but I think that means you're a member of the troop, maybe even an enlisted man, but like I say, I ain't exactly sure." Blue tended to interpret the law liberally. To the best of Blue's knowledge, the five surviving Mexican Rurales taken prisoner during the misunderstanding at the border outpost were the cause of some embarrassment to the US and Mexico. It appeared that neither side wanted to admit what had happened.

The prisoners seemed to be happy working at the post, and didn't actually want to return to Mexico. Within a short time of their capture, they realized that Colonel Mason was a good man, not a thief and butcher, like their former commanders. Mason gave them an allowance, out of his own pocket. Time and again, the Colonel had tried to explain that if they decided to escape and return to their homes in Mexico that it would be all right, but Miguel could not return and dishonor such a man as Colonel Mason. Besides, the maniacal charge of McGuillicotty's raiders greatly diminished Miguel's desire to seek glory on the battlefield. Getting knocked down, kicked in the butt, and marched back to Camp Jones was about all the glory of war he cared to deal with.

"Corporal Blue, you are very wise, but I don't think I want to be an enlisted man again. I am happy with the salary your Colonel pays me for being a prisoner and helping out around here. The other men have talked about escaping and walking home, with the Colonel's permission of course, but I think I will stay here."

The Texan took another healthy swig from the flask then handed it to Miguel. He paused and took a deep thoughtful breath before speaking up. "I hope you do decide to stay. I don't know much about the law like Blue does, but I think the Colonel appreciates how well you all have cared for his quarters and his horse. The boys appreciate them Spanish lessons too. I always thought that it ain't too good to haven't mastered nothing but one language like me."

Miguel took a short pull on the flask and

returned it to Boothe, "My mind is made up my friends. I will stay here at Camp Jones and serve the great Colonel Mason and your Sergeant McGuillicotty. Two finer men are not to be found."

Blue nodded in agreement, "The Army won't see the likes of them again. And I for one hope they let you stay." He handed the flask back to Miguel who raised it in a salute to his friends.

"To the United States Cavalry and its honorable men..."

# Chapter 10

## October 13, 1911 - Camp Jones

At Officers call that evening after dinner, Captain Mason and the officers of the 5th and 10th met to review conditions on the border. Mason held the belief that the instability of the Mexican government would have more than a little affect on the shared borders of the United States and Mexico. Mason relayed his belief to his men and added his suspicions that some form of an invasion or attack from the South was a distinct possibility. The commander at Fort Huachuca, home of the 10th Cavalry, had responded by wire that he concurred. Although the politicians in Washington didn't want to take any action that might disrupt US and Mexican relations any further, the officers stationed on the border posts would do what they had to do.

The first order of business was to intensify the presence of the Army in the border town camps. Roving patrols to stop smugglers would also have to be stepped up.

Colonel Mason stood and addressed his colleagues, "Gentlemen, as you know President Diaz has been overthrown and fled Mexico. The current leader is no friend to us. We must prepare for dealing with renegade armies and the possibility of Mexican incursions into Douglas, Bisbee, Naco, Nogales, and even Fort Huachuca. Our orders are to form a patrol consisting of elements of the 10th and the 5th for a scouting mission along the border seeking intelligence on outlaw border gangs. If prisoners can be taken, debrief them thoroughly, and report the findings to me. Lieutenant Cleary will be in command. The patrol area will be from Naco to the New Mexico Border."

Lieutenant Cleary stood, "If the Colonel please, is there a disposition on the prisoners from the small skirmish Southeast of here yet? "

Colonel Mason lowered himself into his chair "I would prefer not to think of them as prisoners, Lieutenant," Mason smiled as he elaborated. "Washington and Mexico City agree on one thing. These men do not exist. I would suggest they be referred to as guests and encouraged to go home."

Cleary smiled, nodding his head in agreement, "If you have no objection, there is one of the prisoners... I mean guests, whom I would like to recruit as a scout and translator for this mission, with the Colonel's approval, of course."

"If you are referring to Miguel Suarez, then the request is granted. I believe he is just a decent young man who found himself caught in a difficult situation. Please talk to him and see if he is willing to work for his keep, and five dollars a month pay. You are all dismissed." With that, Colonel Mason stood, saluted, and sat down again reading over his papers.

Cleary returned to his quarters. At his simple desk, he worked out the plan of his upcoming patrol. Writing by candlelight, he refined the details. The troops would leave in two days for a month-long mission. The logistics of establishing supplies, equipment, and food had not changed much for a horse patrol since General Crook had been in command of the area in the 1870s. A well planned supply train of mules maintained by professional contract packers kept the soldiers in beans and bullets and the horses in oats.

Unlike the old days of General Crook, the soldiers had some respectable personal firepower at their disposal. Each man carried the bolt action 1903 Springfield in a leather scabbard attached to his McClellan saddle. The men carried either a .38 revolver or a new government model .45 automatic on their belts. To hone their skills the troops took good advantage of an unusually large inventory of training ammunition. All men under

Cleary's command were crack shots, as he was a taskmaster about firearms training. Rumor had it that Cleary himself was able to hit a silver dollar consistently at over 100 yards.

Two hours later, Cleary finished his plans and called for a preliminary briefing of the NCOs in his tent. When the business at hand was finished, he turned in for the night.

By seven in the morning, after two days of training, planning, and preparation, the NCOs had mastered the plan and all appropriate steps preliminary to the point of departure were implemented.

On the parade ground, Cleary mounted up, moved to the head of the column, and gave the command, "*Forward, Ho!* " The troop moved out of Camp Jones and westward along the border to Naco.

## Hermosillo, Sonora Mexico

The revolutionaries organized in Hermosillo, where Garcia led his men to the city square, riding in a loose formation of twos. From his tall horse, he looked down at the peasants and laughed as they scurried like mice from a hungry cat, hiding in doorways, afraid to see or be seen. Obviously, his vicious exploits had preceded him.

Garcia took pleasure in the desperate whispers of the peasants, '*Cuidado, por El Cuchillo*' as he and his soldiers rode down the narrow streets,

He dismounted at the largest cantina in the town, a place traditionally serving as a gathering place for the informal leaders of the Great Revolution. Garcia handed the reins of his horse to his second in command. He strode through the entrance, pushing the double doors hard enough to make them slam against the walls. The smack of the doors was followed by silence as the occupants around the lone table stopped and turned, looking to see whom the intruder might be before they killed him.

Garcia put his hands on his hips and stared into the eyes of each man. He could feel them sizing him up as an enemy. He spoke boldly. "My name is Juan Pedro Garcia, Colonel of the Revolution. I place myself and my men in the service of the commanding general, Francisco Villa." He rested his hand on the butt cap of the eighteen inch fighting knife strapped to his belt.

The man at the head of the table slowly stood. Like an angry rattlesnake he struck, pulling a Colt revolver from a belt holster and pointed it between the coal black eyes of Juan Pedro Garcia. "Perhaps, my arrogant friend, you should tell me why I shouldn't kill you right now? "

Juan Pedro didn't flinch, "Kill me or pour me a drink, I don't give a damned which. Just don't waste my time, pendejo."

The man snorted, as nervous laughter broke out among the men at the table. A fat man to the left of the leader got up and offered his hand to Garcia. "You must be the man they call El Cuchillo. No one else carries that big of a knife and has such a grand impression of himself."

El Cuchillo took the hand. Another man pulled a chair up to the table for him. El Cuchillo heard the man introduce himself as Captain Tesca.

Garcia offered his hand to the thin man at the head of the table. He noticed that the leader's hand was deformed, the thumb was missing.

The leader offered his name as Valenzuela. Garcia thought it was probably an alias. He tried to recall the nickname of a bandit with a mutilated hand he had heard of, but he couldn't recollect. He did not ask. It did not matter. These were the kind of men who didn't care for questions. It was easier to kill a man than to answer him.

Like Juan Pedro Garcia, Tesca and the man calling himself Valenzuela had not yet actually met, or even seen the great Pancho Villa. They were merely a confederation of criminal opportunists, trading on the name of the infamous revolutionary leader, nevertheless their cruel and ruthless criminal ways transitioned well to border warfare. They had gathered a sizable number of men.

Inspired by greed, the outlaws got down to the business of their war. The bandit army needed motivation to advance. It was clear to the all of them that although the Yaqui Indians could be paid in horses and mescal, the rest of the men would move only on cold hard cash.

Garcia spoke up, "Mis Amigos, I have an idea that may solve many of our problems. Clearly we will need more men, horses, and money to meet our goals." He looked around the room at his fellow outlaws, massaging the handle of his knife as he spoke. "I, Juan Pedro Garcia, Colonel of the revolution, and six of my brave men will raid the exchange house in Naco. It should be ripe for the picking. A raid at Naco, with all the cash we will get, might inspire other men to join the revolution. Additionally, such a raid would draw the US. Army and Arizona law officers to Naco, and away from Agua Prieta." He paused again and took a drink. "You General, take all the men to the hills south of Agua Prieta and wait for my arrival."

"Why should we do this? What is in Agua Prieta

for us?" Valenzuela asked skeptically.

"Because, my good friend, there is not a damned thing in Agua Prieta... but on the North side, in Douglas, there is a very rich bank... a bank that is waiting for us to come and blow up the safe. And, there are over a thousand horses in pasture at the edge of town near the army camp ripe for the taking. With the soldados and lawmen scouring the hills near Naco for the exchange house robbers, we will take what we need in Douglas. With the money, men, and horses we will then have, our army can raid both sides of the border at will." Garcia smiled as he slowly lowered himself into a chair.

Naco was an irresistible target for raiding bandits. A small town that existed only for border commerce, it was developed due to the antiquated trails that were being improved into highways connecting Mexican cities to the United States. Naco does not translate from a Spanish word. It was made up by Yankee entrepreneurs using the last two letters of Arizona and the last to letters of Mexico. The capitalists were wise in their choice of towns and the coffers of the border exchange house were always filled with riches.

The revolutionaries could expect only minimal resistance at the Naco cash house, yet they knew their men would sack the entire town, destroying everything in their path. Unnecessary as that might be, it would be good practice for the new revolutionaries; and anyway, there was no stopping an army of ignorant peasants, Yaqui savages, mercenaries, and bloodthirsty killers from doing what ever they were going to do.

Valenzuela considered the idea for a moment and then answered, "Yes... Yes, that is a grand plan,... and I think it will work."

Vesca nodded in agreement, "Yes, very daring indeed, but even if only one portion of the plan works, the outcome is still to our benefit. I think we should do it."

Valenzuela agreed, "Yes, Colonel Garcia, proceed with the raid in Naco. We will be waiting to attack Douglas upon your arrival there."

## Camp Jones

Franky looked forward to the patrol. It was way past time for a change in routine. Camps activity had become boring. He finally settled down from the last excitement at the Rurale border outpost and was able to sleep most nights without the nightmares. As horrible as the events were, he continued to suffer from an unsettling restlessness and desire to experience the incident again, even though he was menaced by the memories in the form of recurring nightmares.

The young trooper was not aware that his body had been subjected to an overdose of the most addictive drug known, adrenaline. He needed another dose. He did not realize why, but he needed to experience the feeling again that comes with mortal fear.

Franky tried to stay busy, so in his spare time he practiced with his new Colt .45 automatic. He tended to fancy himself as a pistoleer. During his cowboy days in Texas, he enjoyed friendly target competition with the other riders from his outfit. Back then they were shooting the old Colt Peacemakers. He got pretty good with the Peacemaker and was pretty savvy about using it. He heard that some years back a local policeman from the area once said that in a gunfight, an accurate shot was more important than a quick draw. Franky believed that was true, although as accuracy was attained, the speed would come. He remembered his first quick shot that missed at the Rurale headquarters and shuddered.

Franky practiced getting the feel of the weapon by moving from a standing position to a draw position a few times, then held the pistol in his hands admiring the design. "This Colt .45 automatic is a real treat for a man who likes guns," he spoke aloud. He heard that some people touted it as the ultimate in handguns. Franky laughed at that *ultimate* talk. No matter how good a gun was he figured someone would come up with something better. It was not that long ago that folks were loading single shot black powder handguns. Decent cartridges were not that new. Franky shrugged. Who was he to predict what would happen in fifty or seventy-five years anyway. By then these, old Colt's would be long forgotten.

Franky enjoyed the practice time. He lined up eight old metal cans and shot them down first left to right, then reloaded a fresh magazine and shot them on the ground right to left. He was getting pretty good, gaining confidence, and improving his skill everyday.

This day was supposed to be a work day though, and Franky knew he had daydreamed enough. He was excited about getting to see the little border town they called Naco on the upcoming patrol. His friend Suarez knew some girls there and Franky was hoping to get introduced to one. Suarez mentioned having a sister, a girl he described as quite beautiful, but the description came with a warning of '*hands off*'. Still, Franky wouldn't mind meeting some of

Suarez' family if the opportunity came up. It had been a while since he enjoyed even the acquaintance of a pretty girl.

After the troop mounted up to move out and headed down the road a few miles, he rode with his pal Suarez, who was serving as a translator, and the old Apache Scout, Big Ugly. The scout was well named for his rough appearance, but his frightening appearance belied the fact that he was a beloved veteran in the horse cavalry. There wasn't a man in the troop who didn't respect Big Ugly's 41 years of service and his uncanny tracking and outdoor skills. Big Ugly could translate Spanish for the unit in most cases, but the Mexican military still harbored a hatred for the Apaches, meaning that Ugly's presence in any negotiations might be counterproductive. Therefore, Suarez served as a translator, as long as the Mexicans didn't check their books too closely and arrest him for desertion.

The mission to Naco was planned with a loop to the North and continued through Sulfur Valley counter clockwise . The troop would set up an observation post in the Mule Mountains and watch for movement through the Sulfur Valley area for three days prior to making their presence known in Naco. Big Ugly would contact an Arizona Ranger he knew from the area and would establish a meeting with Lieutenant Cleary.

## Chapter 11

Young Lieutenant Cleary began experiencing a significant change of attitude about the soldiers of the remote Arizona outposts since the incident with the Rurales. He developed a strong sense of respect for his NCOs and for the frontier soldiers he served with. During the course of his reflections, he accepted that he had been mistaken in his belief that valor and courage were solely propriety to the educated and polished of eastern society. However sentimental the incident may have left him though, he still maintained his distance. He remained Lieutenant Cleary, Officer and Gentleman, to the troops in general. However, there was now a new bond between himself, McGuillicotty, and Boothe. Although seldom seen by the troops, it certainly existed. It was the warm feeling of brotherhood often shared between comrades in arms who faced certain death together.

The troops of Camp Jones had developed a new perspective on Lieutenant Cleary as well. Although he was a little too disciplined and '*by the book*' for the tastes of most of the desert Cavalry regulars, he had proven himself as a fighting man. That earned him some degree of their respect. He still wasn't proven as a tactician and leader of men, but the troops sensed there would be plenty of opportunities for that.

The patrol was uneventful for the first three days. The observation post was set up and numerous scouting missions were conducted throughout the Sulfur Valley. The first real break in the routine occurred when 'Big Ugly' brought in Arizona Ranger Sergeant Bill Peterson to see Lieutenant Cleary.

A sentry spotted them riding in at a slow walk and announced their arrival, the hulking scout and the wiry ranger.

Cleary and Peterson completed introductions and walked over to Cleary's tent to talk. Peterson was young but had a reputation as a good man in a fight. Cleary looked him over, noting the cotton shirt and faded tan canvas jacket that was popular with the local ranchers. The jacket covered the Ranger's gunbelt and part of the holster. His Mexican style spurs clinked as he walked. The wide brim hat with the high crown cast a shadow over the Ranger's eyes as he stooped to enter the command tent.

The Ranger got right to the point. "Lieutenant, We have been plagued over the past six months with outlaw gangs crossing the line burning ranches, and stealing horses and cattle for the so-called revolution in Mexico. I suspect that's just the beginning. I would predict something a lot bigger coming. Maybe a bank or maybe even a run at the remounts at Camp Jones." Peterson spit chewing tobacco on the ground to punctuate his assessment.

Cleary nodded his head in agreement, "Our intelligence provides a similar assessment, Ranger Peterson. Do you have any idea who or what we might encounter here?"

The Ranger nodded, "Six months ago I would have told you the name, Juan Pedro Garcia, a two bit border rat who promoted himself to a Colonel of the Revolution. Garcia, who also goes by the name El Cuchillo, hit a few horse herds a while back. You might have heard about the brutal massacres at some of the ranches along both sides of the border. Men, women, and children killed. I suspected him to be behind it, but word is he headed for Hermosillo with about sixty or eighty men, maybe more. When that murdering bastard gets back, we got us a problem."

Cleary considered the information. "How many men do you have working with you? " he queried.

"I got plenty of help. There are twenty-six rangers in Arizona and eight of us are working the

125

border from Yuma to outside of Silver City, New Mexico."

Cleary blinked as he calculated the distance between the two towns as about 400 miles. "Twenty-six men?"

Peterson nodded, "I know that sounds like a lot of Rangers, but we need every one of them."

Cleary paused at the statement. He suspected that wasn't just talk. He meant it. This cowboy lawman was as tough as they come. "I could not disagree with you, sergeant." Clearly wiped his face with a handkerchief. "Sergeant Peterson, would you consider taking a ride down to Naco, and see if you can determine the current whereabouts of this Garcia fellow? I would like to send my Apache Scout 'Big Ugly, Trooper Boothe, and my translator, Miguel Suarez, down there too. They may be of assistance."

"Glad to have the company, although I'm not real used to it. But the truth is Lieutenant, my horse is done in, and I reckon I am too. If it's all the same to you, can we start out in the morning? " He took off his hat and ran his hand through his thick brown hair.

Cleary stood up and extended a hand, "Certainly, Sergeant, and I sincerely appreciate your help. Please get some chow at the mess and we will tend to your mount." Cleary signaled with a nod for a private to assist the ranger.

Thank you, Lieutenant. I appreciate your hospitality... and I promise, we'll find El Cuchillo. Don't worry." They shook hands and the Ranger left the tent.

Cleary walked outside and noticed Bronk standing nearby, "That, Sergeant McGuillicotty, is one... excuse my language, tough gunslinger."

"Aye, sir, that he is... The territory could use more like him."

"Well, apparently there are already twenty-six of them *just* for Arizona." Cleary smiled and walked back into his tent.

*Daniel Byram*

## Chapter 12

The following morning the odd group, Ranger, Trooper, Indian scout, and Mexican soldier, rode to the foothills about a half of a mile north of Naco. Hunkering down to rest and eat, they developed their plan of action. Peterson seemed to do most of the talking and the others listened out of respect for his experience in this sort of thing.

Peterson asked his companions to execute assignments, rather than ordering them, out of respect for their service. "Miguel, If you don't have a problem with it, how about you and me riding in to town by separate routes and see what we can see. I'll meet you outside the cash house. I figure you and me would attract the least amount of attention there, particularly if Garcia and his bandits are in town.

Boothe joined in, "Me and Ugly will camp at the edge of town on the US side and wait to see what happens.

Ugly had a bad feeling about the patrol. He added his warning. "If anything goes wrong you get back to the border... you get back as fast as you can, and we will cover you."

Boothe looked each man in the eye, "Nothing should go wrong, This is *just* scouting. If we see anything, we have to get back and report to Lieutenant Cleary."

The others nodded in agreement.

Peterson spoke up, "I have a contact in a local cantina who may know a member of Garcia's group... and who, for the right price, might share the information. If he's in town, I think I can find him. Most likely he'll be in one of the saloons that's frequented by the bandits. Most likely the one called the 'El Colonia Cantina'. We'll be back before dark either way and plan our next move."

Boothe gave a light shrug, "You know this country... better than me anyway... just be careful." Franky already was developing an admiration for the Ranger. No uniform, no support, just a badge and a gun in outlaw territory. They finished their briefing, and then Boothe watched as Miguel and Peterson descended from their encampment and headed for town.

Naco

The Ranger entered the bar. He instinctively pushed his way through the door and sidestepped out of the light. He learned at an early stage in his career that there was no sense in silhouetting yourself like a peacock. Peterson took a long look around the bar and stared down any of the riff-raff and criminals who dared to make eye contact with him. He purposefully looked each occupant of the saloon in the eye and let them know through his body language that he was a man ready to fight. Not everybody in the place was a bad man, although many were. Peterson had worked enough border towns to know that it was the one's you couldn't see who were generally the most dangerous.

Peterson sized up the crowd. There was an unusual make-up of this bunch, probably due to the sudden vast wealth that had come into the small town. Instead of just border traders and cowboys, the dumpy saloon was shared with bankers, investors, and cattleman. More than a few bandits were also present.

As Peterson stepped further inside, he was instantly recognized by a patron sitting near the back door, Billy Fargo... border filth.

Fargo recalled the rangers hanging one of his associates for murder about a year before. Fargo didn't care much about the hanging or getting revenge. He didn't even care that the dead associate was his cousin. Fargo needed funds for another drink. He knew who would pay for information about the appearance of an Arizona Ranger in town. He quietly slipped out of the bar and crossed the back alley.

Peterson walked over to a table and sat down. He waited.

Miguel sauntered in about five minutes later through the back, looked around, and the as inconspicuously as he could, joined Peterson at his table.

Within a few minutes, Peterson's contact, a local thief named Rubio, entered the cantina. Rubio clearly wasn't happy to be there. He slowly walked over to them and took a seat at their table. The informer was extremely nervous. "There's trouble here. You should leave. I shouldn't even be talking to you."

Peterson drew a deep breath and let it out slowly through his nose, creating the impression that he had been told the obvious and wasn't amused. "If there wasn't trouble, why the hell would I be in a stink hole like this talking to you, goddammit?" Peterson's face contorted into a snarl.

Miguel flinched as the usually quiet Ranger became threatening and dark, using profanity like a sledge hammer on the informer.

The ranger leaned across the table getting nose to nose with his informant, "You know who I'm looking for... Just tell me if the son-of-a-bitch is in town or not. Then all you got to do is keep your mouth shut and get out of here. Is that too complicated for you?"

The informant sat down quickly and nervously looked around, "You don't understand..."

Peterson glared, "No, you don't understand, you stupid bastard." He reached across the table and grabbed Rubio with his left hand. "You tell me what I want to know, or I'm dragging your filthy carcass back to Bisbee and let the cattlemen hang your scroungy ass. Now dammit is he in town or not?" Peterson let go of Rubio and sat back down in his chair.

Rubio spoke in a whisper, "I'll tell you what I know."

At a nearby tavern, Juan Pedro shrugged when told by Fargo about the lawman. Without any emotion he declared, "Let's kill him. We don't need another gringo stinking up our town, and damned sure not a pinchi Ranger. We'll kill him and dump his body in the desert." He wiped his face with his sleeve and got up from the table.

Six heavily armed men accompanied Juan Pedro Garcia to the El Colonia Cantina carrying shotguns, rifles, and pistols. The seven revolutionaries appeared as stereotypes of the bandits described in the eastern newspapers.

Drooping mustaches, long hair, and dirty. They quietly entered a side door.

No words were exchanged. Juan Pedro walked up briskly and with a pistol in each hand, shot the translator Miguel Suarez in the face and the Mexican informer in the chest.

The ranger dumped the table and returned fire, fanning his Colt revolver into the crowd. Blood sprayed as the heavy .45 caliber Long Colt rounds hit bodies. He dove to the left, then ran out the door, still shooting as he leaped over a water trough.

Franky had heard the shooting, jumped on his mount and rode across the border line with Big Ugly close behind. He saw the Ranger pinned down and the outlaws shooting at him from the cantina.

Big Ugly and Boothe pulled their rifles from the scabbards and began laying down cover fire as they rode. It was already too late. Outlaws came out like cockroaches to join the fight against the trapped American lawman.

The Ranger made his break running about four steps before fire from the saloon dropped him. He was hit several times, yet he continued crawling towards the border.

The Mexicans broke the cover of the cantina and tried to run down the wounded and dying Ranger as he struggled to get back to the US side of the line. Franky pulled his two Colt .45 automatics and charged at them, firing in a desperate attempt to save Peterson. All the attackers turned except one man.

A tall Mexican with a black sombrero stood behind Peterson's prone figure and leveled a Colt at the Ranger, thumbing back the hammer. Peterson looked up toward the border and reached his left hand towards Boothe. The Ranger's brown eyes showed determination. He could make it.

Juan Pedro Garcia pulled the trigger, and the back of the Ranger's head came apart. He collapsed limply in the dirt, three feet from the United States border. Boothe stopped his horse, dismounting as the gelding sat down and skidded to a halt. He leaped out of the saddle and assumed a marksman stance. His hands shook, he couldn't control it. He took careful aim at the murderer in the black sombrero, pulling the trigger on the colt three times.

Two rounds hit the bandit in the upper shoulder, one breaking his collar bone, one creasing the skin. The third round tore off part of his ear. As Garcia fell backwards, his men ripped loose with a hellish barrage of fire directed back at the trooper. Boothe leaped for cover behind a pile of wood.

He quickly reloaded the .45s with his spare magazines. Searching for the scout, he looked over his shoulder in time to see Ugly take aim and fire a shot. The round from the scout's Springfield nearly decapitated one of the bandits. The others ran for cover. Boothe could see Ugly starting to carefully move in closer.

A bandit by the bar screamed, "It's the army... The Americans are coming. Get the hell out of here!"

The bandit leader was dragged away by the others as they scurried for protection from the troopers. The revolutionaries regrouped in an alley behind the cantina where their horses were gathered and rode hard out of town to the Southeast.

Franky shouted across the street to Ugly, "Get the troops. I'll finish here." Ugly took a moment to look at the Ranger's body, then turned and rode off as ordered, his face giving away no emotion.

The hostile crowd had disappeared back into the woodwork, vanishing into the bars and whorehouses of the city after the death of the

Ranger.

It was over. As quickly as it started, the fight was over.

The trooper solemnly kneeled over the Ranger's body. Boothe wasn't heartless, he just didn't cry at tragedy. He still felt it. He just couldn't show it anymore. He reloaded again and then walked into the empty cantina. He sat on the floor with the sprawled remains of his fallen amigo. "I'm sorry Miguel." He placed his hand on the back of the body, remembering the face of his cheerful friend."I got you into this... I promise I'll get you back to your family." He closed the partially open eyes of Miguel Suarez... eyes that would see no more.

Boothe wasn't going to forget the face of the man in the black sombrero. As he lifted Miguel Suarez' body over the saddle of his horse, he made a promise to himself that he would finish the job. Miguel didn't deserve to die like this. Peterson didn't either, but Peterson being a fighting man had accepted the possibility. Miguel was simply a kind, but naive, young boy. Boothe vowed, *Those murdering devils were going to pay dearly for this.*

*Daniel Byram*

# Chapter 13

## South of Naco

The Mexicans rode hard for twenty minutes, then stopped to treat their wounded leader. The stampede string still held the large black sombrero around his neck. Surrounded by his men, the furious El Cuchillo's speech was choppy as he was being bandaged, "Split up. You six meet at Cananea. Get our men there. The rest of you, pick up the men in Nacozari. If they pursue us, we leave too many trails to follow. Meet in three days outside Agua Prieta. There will be other men waiting for us there. I want every rider we have. These damned gringos will pay for this!"

Jose Lopez tore his shirt to make additional bandages. He was wide eyed and trembling, "Jefe, what about you? "

"You have family in Douglas. Get me there now and find a Doctor. We'll take Archuleta too. Get the horses ready." He spat commands as he slowly got to his feet. "Get going now, chico... dammit, vamanos."

El Cuchillo knew pain well. A normal person would pass out from the agony of the wounds that Boothe had inflicted, but not El Cuchillo. Hard as the brutal Sonoran desert he called home, El

Cuchillo mounted his horse by himself and turned eastward as the rest of the band scattered.

Jose Lopez watched with worship in his eyes for the bandit leader. It was clear he would follow the orders of the man he considered a hero. The bandits spurred their mounts and disappeared into distant dust clouds.

## The trail to Naco

Lieutenant Cleary rode in the lead with McGuillicotty and Young on either side. Big Ugly and the rest of the patrol followed at a walk.

They stopped in front of Boothe. He was walking up the road, slowly leading two horses. On the horses were the bodies of two good men.

Cleary's jaw visibly tightened as he stared at the procession He closed his eyes and bowed his head for a brief moment.

Boothe's chin sank to his chest, "I'm sorry Lieutenant. El Cuchillo found us before we found him."

Bronk and Pappy dismounted and took the reins of the two horses from Boothe. They found canvas on a pack mule and wrapped the bodies.

Cleary stared into the horizon. "Is there any hope of a pursuit? "

"No sir... They high-tailed it south, then most likely they split up to the four winds."

McGuillicotty interrupted, "Big Ugly said you got some of them."

Boothe answered, gesturing towards Peterson's body. "He killed three in the bar right off. Ugly nearly took one's head clean off with a rifle shot. I got one, maybe two, but the rest got away. I'm pretty sure it was Garcia who killed the Ranger." Boothe's eyes narrowed as he continued, "Peterson was done in, crawlin' for the border when that bastard came up and shot him in the back of the head like it was nothing." Boothe looked sadly into the Sergeant's eyes, "Dammit Bronk, Garcia should be dead. I hit that son-of-a-bitch in the neck with my .45. It ended the fight, but the son of a bitch still got away."

Bronk put a hand on Boothe's shoulder. There was nothing to say.

Cleary spoke again, "Trooper, would you and the Indian Scout please see to the return of Señor Suarez's body? We'll see that the Ranger gets buried at Douglas and notify his people." Cleary paused, then spoke so softly the others couldn't hear, "And Frank, I'm sorry. I know you and Miguel were friends."

Boothe took a deep breath and let it out. He set his jaw before he looked at Cleary in a new way, "Thank you, sir."

Cleary's next words were a curt order, "Carry on, soldier."

Boothe saluted. He walked to the supply mules to replenish his ammunition and to secure rations for the next leg of the trip.

Bronk approached Cleary and snapped to attention, "Sir, permission to speak freely sir."

"Within reason, proceed, " was the brief reply from the young lieutenant.

"Lieutenant, I respectfully request permission to accompany the trooper on his burial detail. I'm afraid he won't follow orders. I mean, he might not go directly back to the fort."

"With all due respect, Sergeant, Why should I believe, that in any given situation, *you* would follow orders?" Cleary squinted as he thought, that damned McGuillicotty stands with the setting sun to his back on purpose.

McGuillicotty nodded towards Pappy, "Sergeant Young can take care of things here, sir. He's the best NCO I ever worked with, Lieutenant."

Cleary stepped away from his mount and stood nose to nose with Bronk. He spoke softly and conspiratorially, "Take the man's body back to his family. See what we can do for them... that's it, mister...nothing else." Cleary drew a half inch closer and softened his voice but hardened his words, "Now listen to these official orders carefully...No pursuit through Mexico, no killing Garcia in Mexico, no heroics in Mexico... Just meet us back at Camp Jones in three days. Do I make myself clear, Sergeant? I don't want to find out later that you tracked that killer down and violated military regulations. If you did that, you would be on your own."

Bronk stood his straightest. His eyebrow cocked in an expression of understanding "Yes sir. Thank you, sir."

Cleary gave the order, "Carry on, Sergeant."

Bronk saluted, waited for the return salute and did an about face. He marched away with a smile on his face. "I might make an officer out of this boy yet, " He said to himself. "He's shaping up quite nicely, he is."

Cleary mounted up. With a grim smile, he thought to himself, I hope they find that bastard Garcia and kill him deader than hell.

*Daniel Byram*

# Chapter 14

### Camp Jones - Commander's briefing

Colonel Mason slowly closed his eyes and bowed his head, reflecting in silence for a few moments. He paused, them raised his gaze into the eyes of his officers and NCOs, "Gentlemen... Let me be *very* clear about this... we are going to find that devil Garcia... we are going to find him and hang him."

He paused again until he was certain each man gave his full attention, "But... we are going to do it on American soil." Mason gave a scowl that deterred any idea of interruption, "He'll be back, I can assure you... and that is when we'll take him."

He took another opportunity to establish burning eye contact with each man, "Make no mistake gentlemen, these atrocities will not go unpunished. I am understood?"

The men responded in the affirmative, confident that the Colonel's word was good.

Mason continued, "In the meantime gentlemen, I want the men of that patrol to stand down for two days. They are all done in and their mounts need rest. We will organize additional patrols and begin again. I'll have a schedule posted soon. You are dismissed."

Mason sat down behind his writing table and turned his attention to his paperwork.

 The other men filed out of Mason's quarters, but Cleary stood fast. "I request permission to address the Colonel."

Mason turned from his work and surveyed the young officer, "Permission granted."

Cleary began slowly without his typical confidence, somewhat unsure of himself, "The mission was a failure, sir"

Colonel Mason gave no quarter, he glared with eyes afire, the veins in his forehead pulsed with pent up rage, "Don't you dare expect me to pat you on the head and say everything will be just fine, young man... It won't be just fine. What happened out there will never be... just fine. Good men are dead, perhaps unnecessarily. The enemy is still at large." He placed both palms on his desk and leaned forward, "I'm not going to second guess your decisions, Lieutenant. I'm not going to forgive your sins. You were in command. What happened is part of command. Sometimes you fail. If a man fails, he has no choice but to learn how to live with it....You're dismissed."

Cleary was not prepared for the Colonel's blunt reaction. His jaw visibly trembled in frustration and anger. He took a short step back, saluted and left the room.

Mason didn't move. He watched Cleary leave, wishing he could have said anything to the young officer but what the requirements of command demanded. Mason took two deep breaths and composed himself. He bowed his head and said a short prayer at his desk before retiring to bed.


Corporal Boothe found the small cottage on the east edge of Naco without much difficulty. It appeared as Miguel described it, with colorful flowers in front and the string of peppers near the entrance. He paused on the small porch, summoning the courage to knock on the door. His colleagues, McGuillicotty and Big Ugly, remained mounted, waiting on the dirt street.

An old woman came to the doorway and looked out. She saw the body wrapped in canvas slung over the saddle and realized what had happened. She fell to her knees sobbing with sorrow.

Franky helped her inside and sat her down on a small wooden chair. He attempted to comfort her. "Tengo mucho simpatico por su familia, señora, " he tried in his Spanish he learned from Miguel in an attempt to express his sympathy. "Su hijo Miguel, un hombre muy valiente, con corozon

147

muy grande - Mi amigo." He wasn't certain of what he said, but he hoped she understood that he wanted to express how much he and his friends respected and cared for her son.

"Gracias soldado, gracias, " she whispered between sobs.

A young woman entered the room and rushed to side of the old woman, After a brief exchange, she too began to weep, overwhelmed by grief over the news of their fallen loved on.

Boothe tried to address her in Spanish but she stopped him with a wave of her hand, "I speak English, soldier. What happened to my brother? Why were you the one to bring him here?"

Boothe explained the story to her, explaining that Miguel was his friend and comrade.

He began feeling an irrepressible sense of guilt and embarrassment as he spoke to the young woman. He could not resist staring at her face. She was so beautiful. He was unable to conceal his discomfort with his uncontrollable urge to gaze into her dark brown eyes and desire to touch her long black hair, knowing that was not the time or place for such things, not with his fallen comrade outside and in the presence of his grieving family.

Confused and self conscious, Booth excused himself and stepped back outside the door. He watched as the priest walked up to Bronk accompanied by several men from the village who took charge of Miguel's body. He smiled, touched by sentiment as he watched the hulking and rugged Bronk kneel and be blessed.

Boothe turned back again into the doorway and took a long last look at the young woman. He took her hand and said, "Ma'am, I want you to remember my name... Frank Boothe. I'm stationed near Douglas, Arizona. And I want you to know... I'm going to kill the man who did this to your brother."

The woman looked up at him, "My name is Rosanna. I will be here. Waiting for news from you of El Cuchillo's death. Buena suerta, Señor Boothe."

Boothe touched the brim of his hat. He walked out of the doorway and to the street, mounted his horse, then rode south with the scout and his sergeant.

They began the slow, tedious process of tracking. Within an hour they picked up the outlaw trail and followed it about eight miles south of Naco. The trail meandered through harsh land. The day was brutally hot and unforgiving. The group stopped and rested the horses.

Big Ugly dismounted and examined the road.

"Here is blood and torn cloth. They stopped here. It looks like they split up." He looked to the sky and across the horizon. "No buzzards around so El Cuchillo must still be alive. Their kind wouldn't waste time burying him. They'd just strip the body of any belongings and ride on."

Franky dismounted and hunkered beside the Indian examining the trail sign. He looked up at Bronk, "What should we do, Sergeant? "

"We can split up and follow the trails out to see if they rejoin, then come back here and regroup. The trails should probably converge within a mile or so and give us some type of direction. This one trail has three horses together. The rest are all single. The three horses could be their wounded leader and someone to care for him... Then again, maybe not. They're wily bastards, they are, son. I think the Indian should follow that trail and see where it heads. You and I can each take one of the other ones and see if they cross. At any rate we'll meet back here by sunset. No later than dawn."

The Indian agreed. They mounted and rode in three directions.

Boothe followed his trail for about six miles when he saw Bronk about a half mile south of him converging on his path. He stopped and rested his horse. As he dismounted, he retrieved the field glasses from his saddlebags. He glassed the valley to the southeast of his position and spotted the dust cloud. It was a group of maybe six riders... El Cuchillo's men. Boothe moved into the mesquite and waited for Bronk.

Within an hour, Boothe sensed the approach of his Sergeant, but kept his eyes on the bandits. He gave a subtle hand signal... Bronk saw it and approached carefully, walking Mac slowly a few yards to Boothe's left, making certain that he didn't raise any dust or make any noise. Boothe motioned for him to come forward to his position. Bronk dismounted and tied Mac to a mesquite bush with a quiff of grass growing under it. He squatted beside the trooper.

"Is it them Franky? " he asked as Boothe handed him the field glasses.

"It's his boys all right, Sarge, but no El Cuchillo." Boothe looked over to Bronk and smiled, "But I bet they know where he is."

"The village of Mateo is over that next rise. It's not much of a village, but it's the last stop before Cananea. That's another twenty-five miles. I'm sure they'll stop in Mateo for water from the village well." Bronk wiped his head with an old kerchief. He held his sweat stained campaign hat in his left hand.

"I think we'd best just take us a prisoner in Mateo this evening, Sarge. Then we'll go meet Big Ugly... and then we find El Cuchillo." Franky pursed his parched lips as he thought about the situation.

"You know what that means, boy, " said Bronk. " There will damned sure be some killing. Maybe even us this time."

"That Ranger was a good man. Miguel Suarez was my friend. You're right Sargeant. There *is* going to be some killing."

"Frank, it wasn't a year ago that we ourselves were going to kill Miguel. Did you forget that lad? "

"I figure that was war, Sarge. This was murder."

"We're not the law. We're not even in the right country, lad," Bronk warned.

Boothe took his hat off, too. "Whatever we do, it's going to be the closest thing Peterson and Suarez will get to seeing any kind of justice done. I'm going."

Bronk smiled, "I was hopin' you would say that, Frank. There is a little cantina in Mateo. Only store in the village. I hear they have a very delicious drink there called tequila. I've always thought I'd like to try some."

Boothe shook his head and smiled. Bronk had

just been testing him. And he called him Frank instead of Franky. Boothe liked that. Maybe Bronk was considering him as a soldier instead of a kid.

The cavalrymen mounted up and circled north of the valley to come in the village through a shallow canyon, allowing them to arrive unnoticed.

# Chapter 15

**Mateo**

The bandits circled the well and drank their fill rather than seeing to the care of their horses... their logic was based in ruthlessness and cruelty, more horses can always be stolen if these die. Riding the stock to death was not a concern.

After quenching their thirst, they pulled the saddles off their mounts and walked over to a little shack across the dirt road at the base of a hill. It was an adobe structure that had no front wall, just three sides and a thatch roof. Inside the shack was a plank that served a bar, and a toothless old hag waiting to serve drinks.

The bandits bellied up to the makeshift bar. "Tequila for me and my men, old woman, " The apparent leader shouted as he slammed his fists into the makeshift bar. The hag handed them a bottle and the bandits passed it around, each guzzling as much as he could before passing it on to the next man.

"Cien pesos, por favor, " the old woman held out her hand.

"Not for the men of El Cuchillo, vieja. We tax you one hundred pesos for providing you with our protection," said a skinny bandit with a large mustache and a green vest. His remark drew laughter from the others.

"Protection from what? The gringos? At least they pay! " she snarled back in protest.

"No, protection from this, you old shriveled puta," green vest drew a pistol and struck her above the eye with the cylinder. He leaped over the counter and grabbed five more bottles and tossed them to his partners drawing more hoots and laughter. He saw the old woman stir, trying to sit up, so he delivered a brutal kick to her, driving his pointy boot tip into her stomach, laughing as she curled into a fetal position sucking for air. While the old woman convulsed on the ground, he rooted through her apron pockets searching for money. A new voice startled him, interrupting the pillaging.

"Hey boys, do you need some help beating up an old lady? Or do you chicken shit bastards want to try out somebody a little tougher! "

The Mexican turned and saw two men. One tall and lean, and one just plain big. The man on the left had a Colt .45 automatic in each hand. The big man had a Springfield in one hand and an old Colt .45 revolver in the other... soldiers... soldados yanqui.

The lean man turned his head slightly and spit

on the floor. "The good news for you is one of you gets to live long enough to tell us where El Cuchillo is."

Stunned by the unexpected gringos, the Mexicans stole quick glances to one another, each waiting to see what the others would do, none of them wanting to make the first move. Only two of the outlaws could understand enough english to know what the gringos said... but all of them understood the intent.

The big gringo spoke next, "Blast em to hell! "

The Americans fired all four guns at once, their vague image in the darkness distorted by flames and smoke. Three outlaws jerked back and fell limply to the ground. A fourth fell to one knee, wounded, but pulled a pistol. The bandit tried to lift the gun to fire but the lean gringo's third shot hit him in the center of the forehead collapsing him like a rag doll. The big man took aim at a fifth bandit and shot him near the testicles. The bandit fell writhing to the ground holding his wound and yipping like an injured dog.

"I've got our prisoner, " shouted the big man. The lean man heard him. He pointed both Colts at the face of the man behind the bar. They both froze.

"Gringo, what the hell do you want! " screamed

157

the Mexican desperately, his hands outstretched.

"One hundred pesos you piece of shit... or did you not hear the lady." Boothe emptied both pistols into the robber. The bandit slammed against the back wall from the force of the first bullet screaming a death cry as the sustained fire from Colts tore him apart. When both slides locked back on the big automatics, the bandit crumpled to the ground in a crimson heap.

Fifteen feet away, the wounded bandit lay screaming on the ground clutching at the area where his testicles should have been. The big man had him by the collar shaking him and screaming in his ear, "Where's El Cuchillo? Donde esta El Cuchillo?"

"No... No... he'll kill me... I can't tell you."

"You'll never be a man again. You're parts are gone, you filthy outlaw...What do you care what El Cuchillo does? Talk to me and I promise I'll kill you and put you out of your misery."

The bandit couldn't stand the agony, he cried out for mercy but the big man wouldn't let him look to see what he had left. The bandit went limp and answered the question between sobs of agony, "Agua Prieta. Casa de la Señora Lopez. Agua Prieta... the American side... Ayudame... por favor... Ayudame."

The big man paled at the mention of Mrs. Lopez. He looked up at Boothe. "We have to go Frank... We have to go right now! " He let go of bandits collar, dropping the prisoner on the ground.

The old woman crawled around the counter and asked, "What about him?"

"I'll leave it to you. He's not hurt that bad. His imagination got the best of him. You can take care of him if you want." Bronk said.

Then he turned to Frank and shouted, "Lets go, dammit. We have no time to waste."

The troopers jogged back to the horses, mounted and rode east at a high lope.

At the Cantina, the wounded Mexican bandit, rapidly breathing and eyes clinched like slits, carefully examined himself knowing that he had a bad wound. He reached down cautiously assessing the damage. He could feel that at least one of his testicles still seemed to be where it was supposed to be. His flesh was too torn and bloody to determine the damage to the rest of his manhood. He needed help.

He glanced up and realized the old hag was back on her feet, slowly coming around the bar and looking at him with hatred in her eyes. He begged her, "Old lady.... Vieja.... Help me. Get me some help."

"Do you have one hundred pesos? " she asked.

"Yes, yes... and much more if your quick about it ! "

The old lady smiled. She walked over to him, sat down, and cradled his head. "I'll be quick..." His smile turned to a scowl, "Bandido... bastard." She cut his throat with a flick of the wrist, then methodically went through his pockets.

# Chapter 16

**Rendezvous**

At a little after three in the morning, the exhausted soldiers met the scout at the designated rendezvous. Big Ugly squatted near a small fire cooking two rabbits. He stood up and handed Bronk a canvas bucket to water the horses with. Ugly didn't waste words on a greeting, "I found the wounded man's trail. He's going back northeast toward Douglas."

Bronk kicked at the dirt in frustration, "Damn. The bandit was right. I think they're going to Douglas to Rosa Lopez's home. She told me she had a son who ran off, went bad, was running with evil men. Hell, I never believed it would be El Cuchillo's gang though." He looked at both men, "I fear she's in danger, lads." McGuillicotty looked sheepish, "I don't want to start any rumors, but she had some of my things at her house, just laundry is all. She did my laundry and the soldiers too, you know. If El Cuchillo finds a soldier's uniform, he might kill her and the boy too."

Frank looked grim, "The Lieutenant said it was possible they might actually try to steal the remount herd and raid the camp. Do you think he has more men in Agua Prieta? Do you think he would be able to do that? "

Big Ugly didn't say much, but when he did it was to the point. "The colonel needs to know this fast."

McGuillicotty finished brushing his horse with some dry grass and sat down by the fire. He tore off a piece of rabbit from Ugly's crude cooking spit. "Ugly, you have the freshest mount. You will have to be the one to get back to camp. We'll rest our horses and head for Douglas in a couple of hours. We'll find El Cuchillo and then report in from town."

Big Ugly didn't say a word. He threw a blanket and McClellan on his horse, mounted up and left. Boothe looked at Bronk, "He didn't even ask how we found out about Rosa Lopez or what happened to us?"

Bronk chomped on another piece of rabbit, "That's because he doesn't care how we found out. What matters to him is that we *did* find out. Besides that, Big Ugly doesn't lie." Bronk swallowed down some of the stringy meat, "He's not eager to be the one to tell Colonel Mason that we disobeyed orders and killed a bunch of bandits in Mexico... again. If you recall son, we were strongly encouraged to not do that anymore." He pointed to the soft ground near the fire, "Now, you get an hour's sleep and then I will. We have a hell of a ride ahead of us.

Boothe threw his bedroll over himself and laid his head on his McClellan saddle. He was asleep in less than a minute. He didn't dream.

## On the trail

The young trooper was quiet in the saddle, lost in thought. He had a lot on his mind. On one hand, his mood was dark as he considered the injustice of the situation. Why were all the good people being terrorized by these thugs? His one good look at the bandit known as El Cuchillo, Juan Pedro Garcia, was all he needed to see the man had no soul. The look in Garcia's cold eyes as he executed the Ranger haunted Boothe. Two years ago, he would have been terrified by such a man. But now he thought of nothing else but hunting him down and killing him. Frank wiped his neck with his bandanna. Well, perhaps he had nothing else on his mind... except thoughts of the beautiful Rosanna Suarez. In spite of his rage, he thought about her frequently.

But Frank wasn't certain what he felt. It wasn't just lust for an attractive woman. He felt another kind of attraction... something personal... like the need for a home and a family. Boothe took a chaw of tobacco. Hell, he had a family... the United States

Daniel Byram

cavalry. And he damned sure didn't need to settle down. But the doubts lingered.

**The road to Douglas, Arizona**

Bronk McGuillicotty chewed on the butt of a cigar trying to think out the problem. Damn it to hell, why Rosa? She was an honest and hard working lady. Bronk refused to acknowledge his feelings for Rosa Lopez as a woman. He couldn't let it cloud his judgment. Whatever happened in the streets of Douglas would be brutal. There was no other way to deal with the bandits. He shuddered at the thought of something happening to Rosa. He snapped out of his thoughts long enough to speak to Frank, "Let them trot for a while, then we'll rest them for an hour."

Frank squeezed his legs gently and the gelding sped up to a trot, "Bronk, why couldn't we just wire in the information from Naco or Bisbee? It would save us a day."

"These damned bandits have spies everywhere. If the information got out, We'd lose our only chance at capturing the bastard."

Frank nodded in agreement, "I know, but isn't Rosa at greater risk if we wait? "

"That's the hell of it son. That's the cursed bloody hell of it." Bronk looked blankly ahead.

## Douglas, Arizona

El Cuchillo and two of his men entered Douglas in the dead of night with young Lopez leading the wounded outlaw's horse. El Cuchillo, slumped in the saddle, half awake... half sleeping. They slipped silently down the dirt streets until they found the corrals of Hector Madueno. Lopez softly shook the sleeping bandit colonel awake. El Cuchillo grunted an acknowledgement as Lopez helped the wounded outlaw dismount. While the horses were quietly traded at the sympathizer's stables, El Cuchillo sat in a corner of the barn and addressed his small command, "Archuleta, locate as many men as can be assembled. We will meet tomorrow east of Agua Prieta in the foothills."

The ugly bandit Archuleta spoke, "Jefe, you're hurt too badly. You will need time."

El Cuchillo shook his head, "Get me to the house of Señora Lopez and find a trustworthy doctor." El Cuchillo softly touched what was left of his wounded ear and flinched. "By tomorrow, I will be better."

Lopez beamed with pride as he led the wounded El Cuchillo to the home of his mother. He was thrilled to return to his home as a successful war hero with the famous Juan Pedro Garcia, Colonel of the Revolution. Finally, his mother would be proud of him.

"Jefe, we will take good care of you. I know you will be fine by tomorrow."

El Cuchillo ignored the peasant boy.

# Chapter 17

**Camp Jones**

The Lieutenant wasn't a drinker but he suspected this might be a good day to start. Cleary sat in his tent, staring at the cheap bottle of tequila he picked up in town. He had been looking at it for four hours, trying to decide if a drink would inhibit the pain. His thoughts were of the men lost under his command... Peterson, Suarez... Good men... His responsibility.

Alone in his tent, he spoke to bottle. "I'm an incompetent fool. What am I doing here? "

The "harrumph" of a clearing throat outside his tent made him jump. He was so self involved that he hadn't heard anyone walk up.

"Permission to speak to the Lieutenant, suh." A deep southern drawl which could only be the voice of Sergeant Major Pappy Young.

"Please come in, Sergeant Major." Cleary stood up and straightened his clothes. He was surprised by the visit. Since his arrival at Camp Jones, no one had ever visited him, and now the first visitor is the legendary horse soldier, Sergeant Major Pappy Young, in the flesh.

Pappy squeezed his bulk into the entrance of the tent and nearly filling the tiny quarters once inside. "Suh, I hoped you could spare a few minutes and give me some advice on a matter."

Cleary concealed his shock. He wondered to himself, why is a man, with the reputation of being a heroic frontier soldier, a legendary hero of Cuba, here, asking a misfit like me for advice?

"Certainly, Sergeant. We can dispense with formalities this evening. Would you like to have a seat? "

"Thank you, suh." Pappy pulled a short wooden stool over and sat down facing the lieutenant.

"You mentioned advice, Sergeant? " he looked in the brown eyes of the Buffalo Soldier.

"Yes, suh. My men wanted to do something for the Ranger's family, but we weren't sure if he had anyone or not. You knew him best, so I thought I'd ask you. I hope you don't mind."

"No, I communicated with the commander of the Rangers by telegram, and Ranger Peterson had no one. No family… no close friends." Cleary felt a wave of grief and guilt. He fought it back and steadied himself.

"He was a good man, suh. He was doing his job and he got himself killed. He just ran out of luck. It happens out here."

"Do you think it was just bad luck, or the foolish mission he was sent on?" Cleary asked grimly.

"With all due respect, suh, the mission was a good mission. It was good judgment. It's just a hell of price to pay." Pappy scooted closer to the table, "May I speak candidly, Lieutenant? "

"By all means, Sergeant Major."

"Bronk and I have been serving in this frontier for longer than I want to remember. We been in war and conflict all over this land and lands across the sea. We seen old folks, women, and children hurt and dying because of bad men... evil men... It hurts inside to think about it because it's a meaningless waste. But then a man like Peterson, or even Miguel comes along, getting themselves killed too... trying hard to stop bad men from hurtin' innocent people... It was an honorable thing they did. Trying to do good is never a waste. It's just that evil men make the price so high. Those two men had nothing to be ashamed of...and sir, neither do you. In the frontier, hardly anything ever goes just right, but when it does, it feels real fine... and when it doesn't go good, you can't never look back. Bronk and me like it tough. He tells me he thinks you're going to be a hell of an officer out here. As much as I hate to agree with him about anything, this time I think he's right."

The bulky black Sergeant and the tall slender

officer sat in silence for over a minute. Cleary spoke next, "You already knew the Ranger didn't have a family, didn't you Sergeant Major?"

Pappy stood up at attention, " It doesn't hurt to double check." He threw a snappy salute.

Cleary stood straight and returned the salute. As the big Sergeant turned and left the tent, Cleary placed the bottle and shot glass back in the footlocker.

## Douglas, Arizona

Rosa Lopez heard the pounding on the front of her house. She dropped what she was doing and opened the door. She stepped back startled, at first not recognizing her son Jose, covered in filth. He grabbed her by the arms and pulled her outside, "Mama, help me bring our guest into our home."

Rosa looked to her left and saw the bandit Juan Pedro Garcia leaning against her house. He wore a torn shirt, soaked in blood and smelled like a pig.

Rosa objected, "This is not *our* house, Jose... not any more. This is *my* house and you and your disgusting, thieving friends are not welcome here!"

Garcia lumbered towards her and backhanded her across the mouth with his good arm, knocking her off her feet, "Shut up Puta. Keep your mouth shut or I'll kill you."

She fell backward off the small porch and into

her flower bed. Touching her hand to her face she defiantly spit out, "Animal! "

Stepping over his mother, Jose helped his leader in the doorway. He looked down at Rosa's figure on the ground, his face red with embarrassment. "Mother, what is wrong with you? Don't you know who this man is?" He looked at her with disgust, ashamed of her insolence toward the great freedom fighter and defender of Mexico.

She struggled to her feet and turned to run for help. She looked over her shoulder, watching her son and El Cuchillo, as she staggered toward the street. She got as far as the corner of the house when a big man, with an ugly, scarred face grabbed her. She didn't see where he came from. He held her by the hair with one hand and held two bottles of Mescal cradled in his free arm.

Another man was with him. This man was dirty or maybe bloody, in the dark it was hard for Rosa to tell, but he too was frightening in his own way. Rosa could see something in his hand that resembled a doctor's bag, but the man didn't look like any doctor she had ever seen. His eyes had the look of death.

They followed El Cuchillo into the simple cottage. Rosa struggled with the brute who held her, but he was too strong. He dragged her in by the hair, and through her face first onto the floor. She hit the floor solidly. She touched her face and felt blood.

She was stunned, but could hear El Cuchillo order Archuletta.

"Hermano, tie this mujera up and lock her in the pantry."

Maria slumped into unconsciousness.

Jose looked to his hero with embarrassment, "Juan Pedro, Colonel... I apologize for my mother. She is foolish and uneducated."

Garcia looked at her bedroom door. "She'll do ...when I feel better."

Jose bobbed his head in agreement, "Of course, Jefe. She'll do whatever you say. A great man has needs, I know."

Garcia looked at Lopez with disgust. Even Juan Pedro "El Cuchillo " Garcia has never stooped to pimping his own mother just to garner favor with a superior. Garcia stared through Jose with cold eyes as he thought, *I must remember to kill this pendejo weakling.*

He knew he would have to kill the mother anyway before he could leave to join the raids on the international exchange house and the remount corral. He looked back at the pantry and thought of what he was going to do to Señora Lopez when he recovered his strength. She was a treacherous bitch. No respect for men. He would teach her respect before he killed her. He laughed as he thought to himself, *she might even thank me.*

*Daniel Byram*

# Chapter 18

## Camp Jones

Colonel Mason sat at his desk writing requisitions when his aide opened the flap, "Colonel, the Apache Scout, Big Ugly is here. He says he has urgent information. He wants to see you right away, sir."

Mason stood, "Send him in."

The corner of the Colonel's mouth turned down in concern when the Indian soldier entered. The Scout smelled of the trail. His uniform blouse was unrecognizable as military issue under all the dirt and dust. The man appeared near exhaustion.

"Ugly, please sit down, " the Colonel pointed to a chair, then came around the desk and sat with the veteran scout, a man he considered a trusted friend.

Big Ugly nodded in appreciation as he lowered himself into the wooden chair. He wiped his forehead with a torn sleeve. "Trouble Colonel. It's El Cuchillo. He's heading for Douglas. He may be staying in a woman's house, Señora Lopez."

Mason's eyes widened in sudden comprehension "My word, You're not referring to Sergeant McGuillicotty's... *uh*, laundress, for God's sake? "

Big Ugly nodded, "It's her son, sir. He runs with that band. No one knew it. Not even Señora Lopez."

"How did you find this out?" The Colonel stood and walked to the small stove at the entrance to his tent. He poured a cup of coffee for the Scout, an unheard of act in Washington, but not the frontier... at least not between two men who respected each other.

"I found out after we delivered the body of the young Mexican man. I found out then."

Mason figured he wasn't getting the whole story, but what he was getting was what he needed to know. He also knew what he heard from the scout would be true. "Where is Rosa's house? "

"Only Bronk knows. He said if anybody else walked into that area El Cuchillo would know and would run away. He's got Boothe with him and they are going to find out for sure if he's there. Then he will send Boothe to get us."

"Thank you for this report. Please, get an hour of sleep and then meet me back here."

"Thank you, Sir."

The Indian left the tent and went over to the hay stack for a nap.

Mason waved in his orderly and directed him to call his officers and NCO's into conference.

He went back to his desk and scratched out some notes on a piece of paper. As he wrote, he thought out loud, "Thank God the men from the Tenth are still here."

The meeting was charged with anticipation of the capture of El Cuchillo. The story of the Ranger's cold blooded murder boiled the blood of every fighting man in the Camp who heard the tale of the brave ranger and his death. Mason took control of the men with his burning stare. Within a few seconds, the meeting room was quiet.

"Our target in this mission, the fugitive bandit and murderer El Cuchillo, may finally be in the United States. His presence on this side of the line creates an opportunity for us. But, gentlemen, do not forget, El Cuchillo is an opportunist himself. He wouldn't risk crossing the border unless he was desperate. Yet even in desperation, he may try to create a situation to his advantage. We had previous intelligence that he was interested in raiding the remount herd. We also know that raiders, outlaws who are possibly connected to him, have hit banks and exchange houses all along the border. Our problem, as I see it, is three fold: First, secure the outlying corral. Lieutenant Cleary will take five men and set up an ambush there.

Cleary interrupted, "Sir, I feel as though I can better serve...."

Mason slowly turned and looked at the young Lieutenant, cutting him off with a glare. "Mister Cleary, were your orders too vague? " The glare turned into a deadly scowl on the Colonel's face.

"No, sir. I'm sorry, sir." Cleary hung his head.

"Very well. Sergeant Young, please deploy your men in teams and set up ambushes for the Exchange house and the territorial Bank in Douglas."

"Yes, Suh."

I will personally locate Trooper Boothe or Sergeant McGuillicotty and find out where the hell El Cuchillo is. I'll take twenty men under my direct command to organize a capture."

"Yes, suh."

Gentlemen, we don't know what kind of deadline we're facing, so brief your men and be prepared to move out in two hours."

The meeting participants exchanged salutes and exited the room. Mason returned to his tent and prepared to go to battle. He heard heels click outside his tent flap and announcement, "Lieutenant Cleary requesting to see the Colonel."

"I don't have time for a long conversation. Come in and make it quick."

"Sir, it's my assignment. I just have concern as to whether or not you have confidence in my ability. I was wondering why I wasn't assigned to the capture of the bandits?"

"Mister Cleary, I don't have time for this." Mason stood up behind his desk, his hands on his hips. "You only have five men. That's all I can spare. If fifty armed bandits try to raid this Camp and steal those horses I want you, Second Lieutenant Cleary, to kill every one of the thieving devils. I assigned you because I figured you would not allow me to lose a single horse. You are not afraid to fight. You have killed a man in hand to hand combat. You are the only person I know of who seems to have a lack of confidence in Lieutenant David Cleary. Now, get the hell out of my quarters and do your damned job."

Cleary stood silently for a moment, waiting to confirm the Colonel had finished with his tongue lashing... then a slight indication of a smile found the corner of his mouth."Thank you, sir, " Cleary replied as he saluted and went on his way to set up an ambush.

McGuillicotty and Boothe rode up to a desert ranch house just outside of Bisbee shortly after nightfall. The troopers could see the soft glow of a kerosene lantern through the window.

Bronk said quietly, "I know the folks here... good people. A while back we chased some Yaqui raiders of their land who were thieving and being a nuisance. They might give us some water."

The riders made no effort to be quiet as they approached, allowing the occupants be well aware of their arrival.

Booth saw a short older man came from around the back of the house with a long gun at the ready.

"Who is it? Quein es?" he said, challenging the approaching riders in English and Spanish.

"Don't shoot Señor Vasquez... It's me...Sergeant McGuillicotty and a friend, Trooper Boothe." Bronk and Boothe stopped still where they were.

"Dios mio, it's Bronk McGuillicotty." His eyes grew wide with wonderment. A large smile crossed his face as he heartily waved the riders in, "Come in, please. Have something to eat," Vasquez insisted. He called out to his family who were watching from the house, "Maria, it's Sergeant Bronk! Paco! Carlos! Come out and see to their horses."

Frank looked around at the people scrambling everywhere. A man would have thought that Sam Houston himself had just arrived for all the commotion going on. Frank figured this looked like a whole lot of fuss for a fellow who simply chased off a nuisance.

The Vasquez family welcomed the two soldiers warmly into their home. Hot food was quickly served. Outside, Vasquez's sons saw to it that the horses were rubbed down, fed, and watered. When the boys came in after dutifully caring for the horses, Maria ordered them to vacate their bedroom and sleep on the porch so the soldiers could get a night's rest.

McGuillicotty interrupted her, "Thank you, no, Maria, we can't stay. We're trailing a bad man. We will have to get back on the trail as soon as the horses are rested."

Her facial expression displayed sincere disappointment that the family could not provide more hospitality to their guests.

"As you wish Sergeant Bronk," she said with a slight curtsey.

Frank finished the last bite of food and shoved his empty plate back. He rubbed his belly as he looked over at Señor Vasquez, "Sir, thank you for the best meal I've had since I left Texas. I wonder if you could show me a place to clean up some? "

Vasquez waved his hand in a gesture indicating Booth should follow and got up. He led Frank to a wash pan and vase out back. The rancher lit a kerosene lantern so they could see. As he ran a wet cloth over his face, Boothe's curiosity got the best of him, "What was the story with the Yaqui raiders and Sergeant McGuillicotty? "

Vasquez looked perplexed, "What Yaqui raiders? "

"Well then, how exactly do you know the Sarge, if you don't mind me asking," Frank inquired. He was not characteristically this nosey and he felt embarrassed for asking whether Vasquez minded or not.

"I sometimes buy and sell horses with the Cavalry and have done so for many years. I really hardly knew Señor Bronk. But we met and talked a few times at Camp Jones." Vasquez put his hands in his pockets as he spoke while the trooper washed up. "When my boys were small and Maria was pregnant with our little girl, I broke my leg badly, very badly. I was laid up for six months. Word got back to Camp Jones about my accident and before long, Bronk and his friend Pappy Young began taking turns coming out whenever they could and helping us keep our ranch operating. Other soldiers helped too, probably because they saw what those two did for us and they respected them... I asked Bronk once why he helped a man he barely knew. He said he shook my hand once and somehow knew I was a good man. He said good men had to stick together or bad men would take away all that we have worked for here on the border. Strange man, your Sergeant McGuillicotty... Our family can never repay him for his kindness."

Boothe shook his head in wonder, "I guess I really don't know as much about him as I thought I did."

"He's not just the tough fighting man and hard drinker everyone claims he is. He is a good man. We pray for the safety of McGuillicotty and Young at Mass every time we go. If not for their help, I don't know what would have become of us."

Within three hours the soldiers were back on the road. If it wasn't for the horses needing a rest they wouldn't have stopped at all. The chance to eat and rest for a little while had given them renewed energy and time to finish the plan.

Frank had a strange smile on his face as he rode alongside McGuillicotty.

"What the devil are you looking at," asked Bronk.

"What happened with those Yaqui raiders back there Bronk? You never told me the whole story."

"Oh it was awful, laddie. I was on patrol, by myself I was... and I saw the filthy bastards raiding the poor man's ranch. I rode in to see if I could help... like any good soldier would... I received two arrows in the chest, I did, for my efforts. I must have killed and scalped twenty of the bloodthirsty outlaws before the rest ran off. The family took pity on a poor soldier and nursed me back to health." Bronk stuck his chin up in the air as he finished the tall tale, hoping that would signal that the conversation was over.

Booth wasn't finished. "I didn't learn scalping at basic training. Where'd you learn it?"

For the first time in a long time Boothe was grinning widely. A good meal and free entertainment from a master at spouting bull manure was too much to ask all in one evening.

Bronk thought for a second and then continued to elaborate on his story, "Oh times were tough back then, Frank me boy, not like it is nowadays. I learned the science of scalping from Geronimo himself. That was after he took me captive as a lad and adopted me as one of his own, of course," Bronk sniffed and wiped his face with a kerchief taking a quick surreptitious peek at Booth to see if the story was getting traction.

"Well, those were tough times... I guess we

sure got it easy now, Sarge." Frank rolled his eyes but Bronk didn't detect the sarcasm.

"That we do boy... The easy life of the US Cavalry. It just gets easier every day."

*Daniel Byram*

# Chapter 19

## Camp Jones

Pappy Young lined up his men. They stood in a perfect formation with their mounts. Pappy put his hands on his hips and stared for what seemed like an hour, then he spit on the ground. The soft, charming, southern drawl was gone. He barked like a bull dog. "Listen up Buffalo Soldiers. Nobody slacks off until this job is done... and this job ain't gonna be done until El Cuchillo and his border bandits are all dead or stored away in a jail waiting to get a well deserved hanging. I want every damned man ready to fight. Some of you ain't seen much action. Some of you have seen probably too much. Most of that fighting has been on open ground... in the desert, on the plains, on the trail... for some of us, even the jungles of Cuba. This one's going to be different. We're meeting the enemy in a town... an American town. So make for damned sure if you shoot somebody you shoot a god dammed bandit and not a momma and baby in the street. But remember...these bandits are the kind of men who will shoot a momma or a baby. That makes them dangerous... and it makes them evil... So kill every one of the filthy bastards as fast as you can."

Pappy turned and paced in front of the line as he continued.

"Remember men... we are the Buffalo Soldiers. A lot of good men have got themselves killed in the line of duty provin' we're as good as any other soldier. Don't any of you do anything to dishonor those men or I'll kill you and scalp you myself. And then I'll stick your head on a guide-on stick and post it on the parade ground back at Fort Huachuca for everyone to see."

Pappy took a step forward and softened his voice, "But men... I know that ain't gonna happen. There are no cowards or yellow bellies here. You're the Buffalo Soldiers and I know that each of you understands what that means. You'll do what you have to do to make us all proud. Proud of who we are. Proud of what we do." Pappy paused again for effect, "Now... let's go bring that son-of-a-bitch in."

The men went berserk with Indian style war whoops and a chant of Pappy... Pappy... Pappy... Pappy... that continued for minutes until the old Sergeant raised his hand. Silence quickly followed the gesture.

"Buffalo Soldiers.... Prepare to mount." Each man placed a left foot in the stirrup and waited.

Pappy Young gave the next command with

military precision, "Buffalo soldiers... mount up!"

In unison the men stepped up and settled into their saddles in anticipation of the next order.

"Forward...Yo-o."

The men cheered again and headed south from the camp to town. Each man hoping to be the one to earn glory for dropping the bandit El Cuchillo off the roster of the living.

Across the camp, the men assigned to assist Colonel Mason on his part of the mission were mounted and waiting in formation. Colonel Mason's aide had the Colonel's personal mount, a tall sorrel thoroughbred, by the reins outside the Colonel's tent. Mason stepped out of the tent and crossed his hands behind his back. He visually surveyed the grounds noting the dust cloud stirred by the departure of Pappy Young's detachment.

Mason mounted, and took his position in front of the formation. "This will be a dangerous mission. A gang of bandits has murdered a territorial lawman. They have been attacking ranches and homes on American soil murdering innocent men, women, and children. Up to now, they have been hiding like cowards behind a border we can't officially cross. Today, we shall try to find them on American soil, or whatever, in our best judgment, appears to be American soil, and end this travesty."

He turned to his second in command, "Captain DiMarco, take the men to the staging area and wait for me. I'll be taking Apache Scout Big Ugly with me to meet Sergeant Bronkowski and Trooper Boothe to get a situation report." He turned back towards his troopers, "Good luck men."

DiMarco took command of the troops as Mason and Ugly whipped and spurred, racing to the Southwest.

**The East Corrals, Camp Jones**

Lieutenant Cleary had each of his men check out three Springfield rifles and an extra 150 rounds of ammunition, except for Corporal Berkmaier, who was directed to get an extra .45 automatic and the Benet machine gun from the Armory. Each man was further directed to equip himself with two days water and rations. While the men organized their equipment, Cleary studied the terrain surrounding the most remote of the corrals where the largest portion of the livestock was held. Cleary felt that would be the most likely spot for an attack.

He sat on a fence rail with a pencil and paper and sketched out his plan for a briefing. The three scrub oaks on the slight rise to the South would conceal the machine gun and a rifleman. The tree stump to the East would conceal another rifle position.

The small hollow by the broken water trough might provide enough cover for Cleary and a rifleman. A third man would hold their horses in the hollow. His job would be to bring up mounts for pursuit or provide additional firepower, whichever was needed.

Cleary chewed on his lip as he thought aloud, "Three men or thirty men? Hell, we don't have any idea what's coming." It wasn't good.

Cleary decided the plan would have to do. It was the best he could come up with. No matter what direction the outlaws came from, the troopers would let them into the corral area and force them into a crossfire. The only escape would be to the north, which would trap them in Crosswind Canyon. If Cleary could push them up there, he could pin down a thousand outlaws for an hour or so, until help could arrive.

Cleary lit the stub of a left-over cigar. If there were only a few bandits... and if they weren't totally familiar with the area to the north... and if his soldiers weren't overrun immediately... or if the bandits never showed up in the first place... everything would be fine.

Cleary took a long drag on his cigar and then slowly blew a cloud of smoke before mouthing an uncharacteristic profanity.

"Shit."

# Chapter 20

## Douglas, Arizona

El Cuchillo laid on the bed as the Doctor cleaned his wounds and administered a dose of morphine. The doctor, Klause Gerbin, was a German national. No one knew him well, but he was always ready to help the revolutionaries, whether it be medical aid or military advice.

Gerbin spoke as he carefully worked on El Cuchillo's wounds, "You can do what you want, but any movement will cause you pain. I will leave you with plenty of morphine. That should help with the discomfort. The good news is that the wounds are clean... no infection. The collarbone will heal. That ear will heal too, but there will always be a piece missing. Can't fix that."

Gerbin's heavy German accent was difficult to understand as he explained the diagnosis. El Cuchillo didn't like the syringe. Gerbin showed him how to just push the needle a little bit under the skin. The morphine would kill the pain slowly and not put him to sleep.

"Thank you Doctor. Now leave us. We have planning to do and it is best if you are not here."

Gerbin nodded, gathered his things, and quietly left the small house.

El Cuchillo began issuing orders with Lopez, "Get south of town and meet Captain Tesca and his men. They are waiting in Mule Canyon east of Agua Prieta. Have them gather as many guns and as much ammunition as they can. We will need explosives too. Find Tesca and tell him to move at dawn. He knows what to do. Then I want you to pick about twenty good men and bring them here to me. After the raids, we will all head back to Mexico together."

Before El Cuchillo could stiffly turn his head to address Archuleta, Lopez was out the door.

"Archuleta, get me out of here for now. It's not wise to stay in one place for too long. I need some food and some fresh clothes. I want to clean up a little. I think I will come back and have this woman this evening if I feel better." He wiped his brow with his sleeve. "And I think maybe I will kill that pinchi Lopez when he comes back. I don't like him very much."

## Outskirts of town

It was almost dusk when McGuillicotty and Boothe arrived in Douglas. They left their horses and uniform blouses at the home of a friend, Roberto Ruiz, a local harness maker. Señor Ruiz also loaned them old horse blankets that they quickly converted to serapes to hide their identity.

They walked in darkness through the streets of the town until they found a hiding place near the home of Rosa Lopez. It appeared dark in her house. They sat across the street observing for over half an hour.

Bronk whispered softly and broke the silent vigil, "I'm going to see if she's in there. Wait here."

Boothe didn't move. He knew how to follow orders, even those given by a man who wasn't very good at following orders.

Bronk approached the door to Rosa's home and knocked softly... Nothing. He knocked again... then he quietly tried the door. It was unlatched. He looked up and down the street then slowly opened the door, drew his pistol and entered the dark front room.

"Rosa...Rosa... It's me. Bronk," he heard a sound, a muffled whimper from the pantry. He opened the door to find Rosa laying bound and gagged on the floor. His eyes gave away his shock at her swollen face and her bloody lips.

"Rosa, where are they?" He cradled her in his arms as she gently laid her head on his broad thick shoulder.

"They're coming back, Bronk. We must run. There is no time." Her voice was strained with pain and fear.

195

Bronk didn't say anything in response. He lifted her up into his arms, turned, and ran out the door. He looked for Boothe who jumped up from concealment with his pistol drawn.

Bronk called to Boothe, "Be ready to cover us... Let's go! "

They ran between houses and across a side street to a hiding place behind the farrier's shop. They sat in a dark corner, breathing hard, recovering from the sprint.

Bronk tried to make Rosa comfortable. "My God lass, What happened back there?" Bronk asked her as he gently dabbed at the blood on her face with his handkerchief.

"Cuchillo .... and my Jose..." She began to soflty sob at the thought of her son going bad. "Bronk, they were going to kill me. They are assembling men outside of town for some purpose. Then they are coming back to my house." She weeped as she continued, "My son, Bronk. My own son is one of these animals."

Bronk held his rage in check, "Rosa, there are things we must do. We have to stop these men. Can you walk with us? If I carry you, we will draw too much attention."

She wiped her eyes and answered, "Yes I think so."

Bronk put his hand on Boothe's shoulder, "Frank, find Colonel Mason. If Big Ugly made it, they will be waiting for us outside of the Hotel Alba. It's where we always meet when we have business in town. Bring them to where we hid the horses. Be quick."

Boothe didn't argue. He walked off briskly, trying not to draw attention to himself from the residents of the sleepy border town. Bronk walked with his arms around Rosa to support her, and headed back to the Ruiz residence.

Boothe walked through the area as quickly as he could. He quietly approached the rear of the Hotel Alba. As Bronk had guessed, the colonel was waiting there near the stables with the Indian scout and their horses.

Boothe took off his improvised horse blanket serape and called out, "Colonel Mason, its me, Trooper Boothe."

Boothe was surprised when the Colonel called back to him by his first name.

"Frank, what is the situation? "

Boothe related what had transpired. Mason considered the information and made the decision to go directly to the Ruiz house. Boothe doubled up with the Indian on his mustang, skirting the edge of town.

# Chapter 21

## Douglas, Arizona

Pappy Young placed his men carefully in the buildings surrounding the exchange house. Some were in second story windows, some were on roofs. He placed a mounted contingent of twenty men about two blocks away. He stayed with the mounted soldiers and placed Corporal Darden in charge of the ten men lying in ambush.

Pappy gave Darden specific instructions, "When you see El Cuchillo come riding in... go ahead and let them dismount... then shoot whoever looks like the leader. That will be your mens' cue to start shooting and then we'll charge in to run down whoever is left."

"How will I know it's them? "

Pappy had an expression of exasperation on his face, "If twenty or thirty outlaws come riding down the street with guns drawn, that, most likely mister, will be them."

"Yeah, but Sergeant Major, I can't just shoot one in the back like that can I? Without saying a word?"

"Sure you can, this is about justice, not about fighting fair. You seem like a man who appreciates justice... or am I reading you wrong?"

"Yes, Sergeant... I am," he replied.

"Then go and get us some justice, son."

"Yes, Sergeant Major."

Pappy walked over to his horse, put a foot in the stirrup and threw himself up into the saddle. He wiggled in the McClellan and cued with slight knee pressure to bring the horse around. He rode off at a walk and joined the other mounted soldiers.

## Outside Agua Prieta, Mexico

Jose Lopez found the riders. He was shocked at their numbers. He made a guess that there must be almost 150 men mounted and another 50 or more on foot. Most of the men had the hard look of the other border bandits that Jose had come to know that past months. Others he recognized as the worthless drunks and scum from the saloons of Agua Prieta. As he continued down the canyon he saw another large group of Yaquis settling around several small fires.

Jose searched for Captain Timiteo Tesca, finding him near the scrub oak trees at the head of the canyon. Tesca saw Jose at the same time and waved him over, "What is the word of El Cuchillo, Chico?"

"Jefe wants us to destroy this town. He wishes to raid the exchange house and to steal the horses at the soldier's camp at the same time."

"That was our plan, and we have enough men to do it. Is he coming here? "

"No Jefe. His wounds are too bad. He wants me to meet him at dawn in town with twenty men at the home of my mother. He wishes to have you personally lead thc attack on the exchange house with fifty men. He wants the remaining men to move on the corrals for the horses. As many as possible are to go there, ride double if necessary, then steal fresh mounts and take the whole herd. He told me to tell you... You must kill as many of the pinchi gringo soldados as you can. Then we are to drive the herd back here where the gringos dare not go."

"At dawn? "

"Yes, Captain... Now I must go back... I must report to El Cuchillo."

"We will be there in the morning chico, as we planned... and then... we will all be rich... Viva Mexico! "

Jose shouted as whipped the reins across the horse's neck galloping back to town,"Viva El Cuchillo! Viva Mexico!"

A loud thump at the door of the Ruiz residence was followed by the stage whisper voice of Frank

Boothe, "Bronk, open up... it's me."

Señor Ruiz opened the door. He admitted Boothe, Colonel Mason and the Indian scout. Colonel Mason paused in the doorway and removed his gloves. He extended his hand to Señor Ruiz, "My deep appreciation for your assistance, sir."

"I am glad to help my friends," he replied.

Mason looked across the room to Bronk, "What is our situation, Sergeant? "

Bronk was kneeling beside Rosa, holding her hand as she rocked in an old rocking chair. "Not good, sir... El Cuchillo was at her house and he is due back anytime with God knows how many men. If she is gone, he may bolt. They have something big planned but she doesn't know what it is."

"I have twenty men near the edge of town waiting to help apprehend El Cuchillo."

"I don't think we will have time to get them. If he comes to her house and finds her gone, then he's gone too." Bronk looked at the floor, "There's another problem too. Her son is one of them."

"We'll do what we can." Mason pulled a piece of paper out of his pocket and a small pencil then spoke as he wrote, "Señor Ruiz, would you be so kind as to take this note to the cavalrymen assembled north of the ridge road near the pond? "

"I know the place."

"We will take this coward Garcia ourselves gentlemen. I don't think he will have so many men that the four of us can't handle them until the troop arrives."

Bronk grimly looked into the Colonel's face, "We've faced more... with fewer."

Mason smiled, "That we have, Sergeant. Now, let's go."

# Chapter 22

Juan Pedro 'El Cuchillo' Garcia took two large gulps of Mescal before he slipped the syringe slightly under the skin of his left arm. The shack he was resting in belonged to an old friend. He felt reasonably safe there. "Archuleta, How much longer until the men should be coming? "

"It will be dawn soon, Jefe."

"Then help me get to my feet. I want to go see Rosa Lopez." A sick smile showed his rotten teeth.

"Do you feel up to that, Jefe? " Archuleta's face gave way to an expression of disbelief.

"I always feel up to it... Especially just before we burn a gringo town."

Both bandits laughed out loud. Archuleta helped El Cuchillo to his feet. El Cuchillo placed his good arm over the shoulder of the big man and they walked the short distance back to the Lopez house.

Mason and his small group rode to within a quarter mile of Rosa's home before stopping to continue on foot. They carried their rifles with them as they made their way quietly through the alleys until they reached an old shed from where they could see the back of the house.

Mason whispered to Bronk without taking his eyes off of Rosa's home, "It all looks dark up there. Do you think he's inside? "

Bronk answered the Colonel, "He's a sly one, sir. He may have moved to another house nearby and be watching this one. He may have gone to do something and will be back here soon, or maybe he came back and found her gone already. My guess is, unless we missed him, I don't think he's back yet."

"I agree. Lets wait here for the time being and see what happens." The Colonel leaned back against the shed. "But I got a feeling," he looked at the other three men, "that all hell is going to break loose." His eyes hardened, "And God help me, I hope I'm right." He rammed the slide back on his .45 automatic and jacked a round into the massive chamber.

Frank Boothe didn't really know the Colonel, but he was getting the impression that Mason had orchestrated events intentionally to get himself in the middle of a serious gunfight. Boothe wondered if Mason was from Texas. He damned sure wasn't the typical officer that Boothe knew from back east. Boothe made eye contact with Bronk and permitted himself a knowing nod. He had no doubt that McGuillicotty wanted to fight. It was personal for him, too. Beating Rosa Lopez was a foolish thing for El Cuchillo to do. That mistake would probably prove fatal.

The trooper stole a glance at Big Ugly. The Indian was stoic. Boothe didn't know how to interpret his intent. Maybe the Indian liked it that way. At any rate, Bronk and the Colonel both respected the old scout and that was good enough for Frank Boothe. He just hoped he'd get his chance to finish what he started in Naco. He wanted revenge for the deaths of Miguel and the ranger. And he wanted to fulfill his promise to Miguel's sister.

Bronk McGuillicotty grew impatient. The chances of catching El Cuchillo were diminishing by the minute. He tried to concentrate on the job at hand but his thoughts kept going back to Rosa Lopez. The affection he felt for her was far more substantial than he wanted to admit to himself. He knew he wouldn't be in the horse cavalry forever. Someday he would have to settle down. He needed his options. If he didn't lose his life on the battlefield, he damn sure didn't want to grow old alone. He wanted Rosa to be with him.

Bronk forced himself to remain focused. If he

started thinking about her, he wouldn't be thinking about fighting. He had to keep his mind straight. He had to concentrate... El Cuchillo, encroached in Rosa's home, struck Rosa, and terrorized her... and if she hadn't escaped he would have done far worse. Think... Focus... Concentrate... Kill El Cuchillo... Kill everybody with him... Kill them all.

Big Ugly served as an Army scout for almost as long as he could remember. As he waited for the fight, he reflected silently about his circumstances. The years with the horse soldiers had been good. The men treated him with respect and were willing to learn about his people and his ways. Ugly liked working for the Colonel. He had served with him for many years, long enough that Mason's enemies were now his enemies, and his enemies were Mason's, as it should be with warrior brothers.

He watched as young Boothe checked his weapon and equipment. The boyish soldier was wise for his few years. He followed in the path of good men. Too many young men follow the bad man's way. Ugly admired how quickly Boothe picked up the tracking skills he showed him. He was learning. He would be a good soldier.

Ugly lastly turned his attention to his old friend Bronk. Sergeant McGuillicotty was known to everyone in the territory as a great fighter. He was funny too. When the Indian was alone, and no one could hear him, he sometimes laughed when he thought about things the big Sergeant said or did. Yes, this was good company to serve with. He was ready to fight. He was ready to die or kill. Either way, it was good to fight alongside such men as these.

*Daniel Byram*

## Chapter 23

The bandits were closing on their assigned destinations. The group of men preparing to attack the corrals consisted of about one hundred of the most vile and evil scum from south of the border. Most of them were mounted, but many rode double or were on foot. They were armed with rifles and pistols for the most part, although some carried only crude spears.

They were led by a vicious border killer and self appointed General of the revolution known as Cuatro, who was a little under six feet tall and very thin. He was easily recognizable by his unusual appearance. He had pinched the top of his right thumb off in a roping accident while stealing cattle. He was usually clean shaven, but wore his dirty hair long and long and tied back by a bandanna. Bandoleers were draped over his shoulders and he carried two Colt Peacemaker pistols.

As the sun was breaking over the horizon the unruly mob approached from the south, raising a slight dust cloud as they moved.

He lowered the field glasses from his eyes in astonishment, "holy hell!" Lieutenant Cleary raised the glasses again and confirmed his worst fears, "There must be a hundred of the son-of-a-bitches coming, " he whispered aloud. His clever ambush on a few rustlers had become a disaster before it started. Cleary rubbed his eyes. The special characteristic that make a man an officer subconsciously kicked in, as the young lieutenant forced himself to control his shaking hands and focus. He already knew the situation was totally hopeless. The fight was lost before it began. They would be killed to the man within fifteen minutes and the herd stolen. His only alternative was to change the game. Cleary barked an order at the horse holder, "Bring the mounts here now! " He shouted directions to his small detail, "grab your weapons and mount up ... NOW! "

## Outside the Lopez home - Douglas, Arizona

Frank Boothe squinted in the breech of dawn light through the dying night haze as he stared down the empty street. He thought he detected movement. He did. He put his hand on McGuillicotty's shoulder, "It's them, Bronk. They're coming."

McGuillicotty nodded, "Just the pair of them, it looks like."

Boothe looked over to Colonel Mason for direction. He followed Mason's hand signals and moved over to a large water barrel at the corner of the house. He looked for the Scout. Across the street behind a woodpile, the Apache revealed his position to his fellow soldiers with a small surreptitious movement of his hand.

Boothe, Bronk, and the Scout waited for the signal from Mason to make their move. Boothe attempted to stay calm by forcing himself to breath slowly. As El Cuchillo walked to within sixty feet, Boothe thumbed the safeties off his Colt .45 automatics. He readjusted his grip on the pistol in his left hand. He was ready.

El Cuchillo had lived a long time as an outlaw by relying on an innate ability to instantaneously respond to his gut instincts. He never tried to think too much, just react in the face of potential danger like an animal. Even with the tequila and morphine he had used, he was still able to perceive that something wasn't quite right. He spoke in a tone barely audible to Archuleta, "Be careful, when something happens move to the right."

Archuleta had ridden with El Cuchillo for many years. In that time he had come to rely on the uncanny instincts of his leader. His unhesitating response to El Cuchillo's orders had kept him alive in many dangerous situations. He said nothing and prepared to move in the way he was told.

Colonel Mason stepped out from around the corner of the barn. He took a target shooter's position with his shooting hand extended and his other hand on his hip. His campaign hat was tilted at an angle that revealed only a portion of his eyes. He drew a bead on the forehead of El Cuchillo. "Don't move Garcia. You are a prisoner of the United States Army."

The grubby bandit slowly raised his hands in a gesture of surrender and smiled. "Jefe, Yo no soy bandido, Yo no hablo Ingles...Esperete uno momento, por favor... Tranqilo."

As Mason began to respond with another command, El Cuchillo quickly moved behind Archuletta, shifting to the left as Archuleta moved to the right. Mason's first shot snapped back the head of Archuleta and sprayed red fog over El Cuchillo. El Cuchillo held Archuleta as a shield while moving to cover behind a shed.

Mason emptied his magazine striking the dead body of Archuleta six more times but the slow moving, heavy 45 caliber rounds did not pierce through Archuleta's body. El Cuchillo dropped the body and pulled his pistol returning fire. Mason dove to the ground taking cover under a cart.

Bronk was shocked at the bandit's quickness.
He took two shots but missed both times. He
regretted not using his Springfield. That rifle
would have plowed a hole through the shed that El
Cuchillo was hiding behind. From the corner of his
eye, he caught hand signals from Mason. The
Colonel was directing the Scout and Boothe to
flank the bandit. He saw Mason make eye contact
with him. Mason mouthed the words "Wait there."
Bronk flattened himself out into the smallest
target he could be. He set aim on the last place he
saw the bandit and waited for the next move.

Boothe initiated his flanking maneuver. He was
moving slowly, totally aware of the dangers
involved with facing a man like El Cuchillo. He
edged his way up the street, never revealing
himself, using cover as he moved.

He looked for the Indian but couldn't see him.
He knew he was there somewhere. He paused and
listened. He felt alone. No one made a sound. No
one was moving. The street was deathly silent
after the initial burst of gunfire.

Then Boothe heard it... the sound of
thundering hooves. From the sound of it, the riders

were about a quarter mile away and riding hard. The rest of Mason's men were arriving and they would make short work of the bandit and murderer "El Cuchillo." Frank balanced himself on the balls of his feet ready to spring when the cavalry unit stormed around the corner and forced El Cuchillo into the open.

Frank's speeding thoughts suddenly hit a wall of realization. The riders are coming from the wrong direction. He looked over his shoulder toward Bronk and the Colonel. Their mouths opened in shock.

Twenty riders cleared the corner and entered the street at a gallop. Frank heard El Cuchillo yell for help in Spanish. The riders were already shooting at shadows and firing in the air.

Mason screamed, "Let the bastards have it! " as he kneeled from what little cover was available and blasted the lead riders as they bunched up in the narrow street. The Americans put forth a sudden and unexpected burst of fire that stopped the charge and created chaos in the outlaw ranks.

The Mexicans fired blindly at all directions without immediate effect, other than to prevent any movement by the Americans. El Cuchillo broke cover and ran into the group of bandits grabbing the horse of a dead rider. El Cuchillo shouted orders, "There is only a handful of them. Take them! "

Frank jumped from his cover and ran towards the Lopez house. A bullet grazed his buttocks causing him to stumble and fall. The bandits tried to ride him down like a pack of jackals attacking a wounded gazelle. Frank rolled to his side and emptied both of his .45s in a deadly burst killing men and horses as they fell around him on the ground. Instinctively, he pushed the magazine release buttons and the empty magazines dropped out of the grips. He slammed in fresh magazines in, reloading in under three seconds. Then a downed wounded horse to his right kicked its hind legs in death throes, striking Boothe solidly in the back knocking the wind out of him.

Boothe sucked for air but couldn't get any. His eyes bulged as the pain swept him. He fought panic. He rolled to his back and lifted his guns for another fusillade into the mob of riders.

McGuillicotty saw Boothe go down. He wasn't sure if he was killed or not. He tried to fight his way to him. A pistol shot from a mounted bandit hit him in the left shoulder causing McGuillicotty to fall to one knee. Bronk saw who shot him. He looked down his front sight, exhaled half a breath, and softly squeezed off a round that hit the bandit between the eyes, rolling him backwards off his saddle.

A wounded bandit on the ground lurched up on Bronk's right and stabbed him with a small knife. Bronk swung his pistol around and hit the bandit on the head, again and again, until the outlaw's skull was soft and covered in red.

Mason had reloaded for the third time, slamming his last magazine into his .45. He edged out from cover to pick up a rifle out of the scabbard hanging on a dead horse. His arm and head suddenly felt as though they were on fire. A penetrating pain caused him to fall forward and collapse. He thought he might pass out but his will to survive overcame his pain and he reached for the rifle absent any conscious effort and retrieved it. He crawled back to cover. Wiping blood that was pouring down his forehead with his forearm, he took aim at the closest bandit and commenced firing.

## Chapter 24

Tesca could hear the burst of gunfire across town. He lifted his rifle over his head, "That's the signal... Let's Go!" Tesca led his small army of bandits down the street to the exchange house. The riders were screaming and shooting as they charged.

Tesca screamed too. "Viva Mexico, Viva El Cuchillo, Adalente...Adalente! "

The bandit was amazed at the brilliant planning of Colonel Juan Pedro Garcia. There was no resistance whatsoever as the robbers rode to the front of the exchange house. This was going to be easy... a great victory. They would all be rich men.

The bandits stopped in the front of the stately building. About half of them dismounted. Of those on foot, most took up defensive positions, while four of the group set explosives against the heavily fortified front doors facing the street.

Tesca looked up and down the street... still no resistance... he grinned. The gringos are afraid. Their cowardly soldiers were hiding in their camp. He lit a cigar as the explosives were being set. Then he saw it... the crown of a brown campaign hat over the false roofline of the building across

219

the street.

The cigar fell out of his mouth as he mouthed the words, "Son of a bitch"

**Exchange House, Douglas, Arizona**

Trooper Darden lifted his 30-06 over the roof line and took quick aim. He made eye contact almost instantly with an ugly man with a cigar in his mouth. The man looked like he spit out his cigar and mouthed some words.

The young trooper squeezed off a round. Darden winced at the familiar pain as the powerful recoil absorbed into his shoulder. Over the sights he saw the head of the bandit disappear. A headless corpse rode the bucking horse for a second or so before falling limply to the ground. Darden heard the bugle call for 'Charge' as Pappy Young led his mounted Buffalo soldiers in a saber charge into the midst of the bandit hoard.

Trooper Darden operated the bolt and found another target. He missed... but killed a horse. He pulled the bolt again and fed another round into the chamber.

Darden saw Pappy Young slashing his way through the bandits with his saber, splitting the group in fragments. The riflemen were picking off the bandits as the group scattered in confusion and panic.

Darden worked the bolt and found targets again and again. He gut shot a man, ripping him from the saddle onto the ground. He missed another, then saw one running from the fray. He hit him in the back of the head at about sixty yards, slamming him face down in the dirt.

The trooper felt a burning sensation on his face. A round hit the wooden facade he was behind driving six inch splinters piercing Darden's cheek. He could barely feel it. He kept shooting.

Pappy Young took his reins in his teeth and galloped into the midst of the bandits. He held his saber high, bringing it down on any bandit neck he could see. He held his old revolver in his left hand, firing as targets presented themselves. He noticed that the bandits seemed to be in a state of confusion. The ambush had provided the troopers with the element of total surprise.

He saw a bandit take a quick shot at him, but he could immediately tell it would miss. Bracing himself in the McClellan, he took an aimed shot and hit the bandit in the center of the chest.

Pappy felt a burning sensation across his belly. A shot from the other side ripped him across the fat of his gut. He ignored it and took a swipe with the saber across the throat of the bandit opening

221

the jugular and spraying blood into the thick cloud of dust.

He rocked forward as a light load of shotgun pellets hit him across the back. Pappy stuffed the pistol in his belt. He turned his mount, spinning to the right with knee pressure and a slight tug of the reins. He saw the shooter sitting on a small pinto. The bandit was trying to reload a double barrel shotgun while mounted on a skittish horse. Pappy sank spurs and bellowed his war cry. The cavalry mount laid back its ears and plowed into the side of the smaller pinto. The bandit and his horse tumbled over sideways. Pappy trampled them both to death as he rode over the top of the jumbled mess.

Ignoring his wounds, he turned back into the middle of the battle. Releasing the reins again, he swung his saber with both hands. Like a madman he slashed and hacked his way through the chaos.

Pappy broke through the crowd into the opposite side of the street. He turned to charge again. He drew the pistol as the horse was spinning.

He stopped suddenly. The carnage had slowed. Most of the bandits were dead. A few wounded littered the ground. Several bandit survivors were riding hell bent down the street to escape. They were pursued by US cavalry troopers. Pappy started to slump in the saddle. Then he saw it, the burning fuse.

Cleary's men scrambled to his position carrying weapons and ammunition. He stood straight and tall as he calmly gave them their new orders.

"Troops, the outlaws will be here in five minutes. If we want to live we have to move fast." He pointed to the trooper who had been holding the horses, " Get as much of the weapons and ammo as you can carry up into Crosswind Canyon." He looked to the rest of the troopers, "Our only hope is to stampede the herd before they can steal it, take them into Crosswind canyon, and hold out until the Colonel gets back here. Let's go "

No one wasted time on discussion. Troopers leaped on their mounts and scrambled to the main gate of the corral. The experienced cowboy-soldiers had the herd stampeding north into the box canyon within three minutes.

Cleary continued to glass the enemy approach. The Mexican bandits increased their speed. It was going to be close. Cleary grabbed his extra ammunition and jumped on the back of his horse.

He quickly turned and joined the herd in the race to the Canyon.

The lieutenant leaned slightly forward in his McClellan and released the bit pressure in the horses mouth. He placed his tongue at the back of his lower teeth and made a hissing noise like a snake, "pssssss." The long legged mount stretched out and ran like lightning, taking him ahead of the herd and to a rocky point at the mouth of the canyon.

As the big gelding skidded to a sliding halt at the point, Cleary stripped the saddle and headstall off the winded horse and slapped it across the butt. He saw out of the corner of his eye that it joined the herd in the canyon.

Cleary glassed the approaching bandits again. They had fallen behind. He did a quick calculation in his head and decided he had about five minutes to set up a defensive perimeter. He gave a hand signal to Berkmaier. Cleary wanted the machine gun mounted high in the rocks to place a sweeping fire over the approaching bandits. He also wanted to be able to discourage any flanking movements. To be flanked would mean a quick end for the handful of defenders.

As the other men reported, he placed them at twenty yard intervals across the narrow mouth of the canyon. Too thin a line to hold for very long, but it was all he had.

Cleary took a last drink of water from his canteen before the fight. The lieutenant quickly started piling stones and building the best cover possible. His hands still working, he stole a quick glance across the mouth of the canyon at his men as they dug in. This was the best he could do. It wasn't enough, but it was their only hope.

Cuatro raised his hand in a signal to halt. The bandit leader was confused by the sudden movement of the herd from the corrals. He suspected a trap. He placed his left hand on the horn of his saddle and twisted in the seat, "Sergeant. Get those boys from the Yaqui village that are on foot. Send them up that wash and to the canyon where the horses went through. The Soldados might have a little ambush set up for us. I don't want to waste any of my horses. Send the Yaquis.

The Sergeant trotted to the rear and ordered the Indians to move forward. Most of them were armed with old black powder rifles and spears. As the Indians advanced, Cuatro organized about thirty riders, "Listen to me, my revolutionaries! If these Indians draw fire from the soldiers, I want you to sweep down from the west and flank the bastards. Get ready to charge at my command."

Cuatro had his Sergeant line up the remaining riders for a lightning charge down the mouth of the canyon, to be launched after the Americans had wasted ammunition on the Yaquis and his outriders had flanked them. The herd of horses would soon be his and the soldiers would soon be dead.

Lieutenant Cleary saw what was coming but he was confused as to why they came on foot. "I'll be damned," he whispered, "they are going to probe our positions to find weak spots and then make their plan of attack. I was hoping for a blind charge. Shit."

He gave a hand signal to Berkmaier to hold his fire. Cleary wasn't ready to reveal the machine gun to the outlaws. He low-crawled to the position of the man on his left.

Cleary whispered directions, "I only want two of you to start picking those outlaws off. I don't want to reveal our limited strength. You can start now." He continued to crawl as he heard the loud report of the Springfield. He advised the remaining men of his plan and designated another shooter. He tried to instill some confidence and put a good light on the situation as he spoke to the men. "Don't worry... Colonel Mason will be here damned quick. We can hold out. As soon as the Colonel realizes that the target was the corrals and not the exchange house, they will come a-running."

Cleary returned to his position and watched as the two riflemen began systematically picking off the attackers as they made their way forward through the boulders and mesquite. The initial volley had slowed things down. The Yaquis were now using cover, crawling through the rocks, more cautious in their approach. Cleary counted fourteen enemy casualties. His confidence grew.

Cuatro was livid at the slow lurching movement of his forces, "The pinchi gringos left two men behind to try to stop us. His face flushed red. "Fools! " he growled. He spat his words at his Sergeant, "Let them waste the rest of their ammo on the yaquis then we move."

His gaze turned again toward the fight. "Tell the men to dismount and rest the horses." He pulled a bottle of tequila from his saddlebag and took a long drink.

*Daniel Byram*

# Chapter 25

**Lopez residence**

Bronk reloaded from cover. He took a deep breath and then peeked around the corner searching for a target. "Where in blaze's name did all these bloody bastards come from?" he muttered.

He got on his belly and crawled towards a better vantage point as he attempted to make a more accurate survey the situation. Mason was down but still fighting. Boothe was down and quiet. The Scout was hidden from view. McGuillicotty knew the old Apache well. He figured the old scout would not break cover until he had a clear shot at El Cuchillo. After all, that's what they came here to do, and the scout was a very focused man.

Bronk took a quick peek from around a tree, confirming that the bandits had scattered to cover, but were still engaging them in hellish gunfire. Although most of the bandits were dismounted, their horses ran chaotically in the street.

Bronk yelled at Boothe, "Frank, dammit boy, get out of there."

There was no response.

McGuillicotty heard the Colonel call to him,

"Get Frank, I'll cover you."

Bronk saw the Colonel pick up an outlaw's rifle and take aim on one of the bandits. The hulking sergeant made a short dash to within fifteen feet of Boothe when the onslaught of fire from the bandits stopped him cold in his tracks. He crouched behind a barrel, trying to squeeze cover out of an object that was just to small to protect the big man. But he was close enough to see the downed trooper now.

He stared hard at the prone body of Frank Boothe for several seconds... Then he saw it...A wink of the left eye.

McGuillicotty hollered across the din of noise at the Colonel, "He's deader than a doornail Colonel Darling. We have to fall back."

He could see that Mason didn't get the hint. Mason just nodded and opened up with more cover fire.

McGuillicotty and Mason backed their way up to the barn behind them and concealed themselves behind a pile of adobe blocks.

Mason looked at McGuillicotty quizzically, "How did you know he was dead?"

Still firing, Bronk responded with a grin, "Oh he's not near dead yet, sir. We need to draw those murdering bastards closer to us and let Frank and

Ugly do their job."

Bronk saw the twisted smile on Mason's face. Bronk pulled a white handkerchief out of his pocket and tied it to a stick. He waved it above his head.

Mason shouted, "We're out of ammo... We surrender. We want to come out."

El Cuchillo had withdrawn his men to the small house across the street from the Lopez house. He spit on the ground in disgust when he saw the flag of truce. "Look at these stupid gringos now," He pointed and laughed. "When I give the signal, we rush these cowards and put them out of their misery."

He leaned slightly around the corner and shouted at the American soldiers, "I recognize your flag of truce, and accept you surrender. Please come out and show yourselves. We won't shoot. You have my word as a Colonel of the revolution"

Mason whispered to Bronk, "I don't think I trust his word... do you?"

Bronc grinned, "Not particularly, Colonel. I suspect the man is being less than honest with us."

"Let's find out, sergeant."

El Cuchillo heard a deep booming voice with a

strange accent, "Hold your fire, blast you. We're coming out now, laddie."

El Cuchillo turned and grinned at the other bandits, "Let them come out a few feet. I'll give the signal. Then you can shoot these gringo soldados.

Mason and Bronk divided up their remaining ammunition and added what they could gather from the nearby bodies.

Mason queried Bronk, "What do we have left? "

"Not, much, sir. But plenty enough to handle these mangy alley cats."

Mason took an old revolver and loaded it. He put his last six rounds of .45 auto in an empty magazine and slammed it home, racking one in the pipe.

Bronk had enough to fully load his .45 and he scrounged up a sharp machete off the body of one of the bandits. They stashed the weapons in their belts behind their backs.

Mason smiled at his old friend, "This is it, Bronk. Is your young Trooper Boothe up for this sort of thing?"

"Oh, don't worry about the lad, Colonel... If we start it, he'll certainly finish it for us if need be."

"Let's hope we finish this ourselves. Of course, you are starting to get up there in years." Mason moved around positioning himself to get up.

Bronk's brow wrinkled, "That I am, sir. Maybe I'll just limp back to the old soldiers home and forget about all this awful fighting." Bronk raise himself on one knee.

Hands raised slightly, with palms forward in a sign of surrender, they gave up cover and came out.

Frank wasn't moving. He knew that Bronk wouldn't quit fighting unless he had the same idea... lure El Cuchillo out into the open, then put him down. Boothe had both his .45s fully loaded and off safety. He permitted himself a slight peek at the street and saw the Mexicans moving forward. He noted that El Cuchillo was cautiously moving behind his men. Boothe closed his eyes and waited, listening to the movement and biding his time.

Bronk estimated twelve bandits still alive and fighting, and El Cuchillo made thirteen. Then he saw Rosa's boy walking with El Cuchillo, cocky and arrogant.

Bronk's heart was torn for Rosa. He knew she wanted him to try to save the boy although he was certain that in her heart she knew the lad was beyond redemption now. Still, even though he knew the death of the boy meant the end of any hopes for a life together with Rosa, her son's chances of getting out of this alive were unlikely. Bronk was torn between his affection for Rosa and his overwhelming urge to kill the boy for what he and El Cuchillo had done to her.

The boy was a weakling and a coward, yet Rosa wanted him spared. Bronk couldn't fathom why. A mother's blind love was beyond his realm of understanding.

He pushed his torment aside and focused on the task at hand. He took a deep breath and moved forward. It was good to be side by side with Mason in battle again. Maybe this would be the last time. Then none of this agonizing would matter.

Boothe heard the bandits strut past his position and he cautiously opened his eyes. He saw El Cuchillo from the back and suspected the kid with him was Rosa's son. The kid was in the way, but Boothe figured it was now or never. He sprang to his feet and gave a warning to draw attention away from Mason and Bronk, "El Cuchillo, drop your gun."

Like a cat, El Cuchillo made a quick spinning movement to his left and placed the boy between him and Boothe. Boothe hesitated. The Indian scout didn't. A 30-06 round fired from his concealed position hit El Cuchillo directly between the shoulder blades dropping him like rock.

Mason and Bronk drew weapons and emptied them into the confusion. Boothe did the same. The Indian gave up his position of concealment and ran into the mob of revolutionaries with a knife and pistol.

Still outnumbered and out of ammunition, Mason and Bronk ran forward with whatever they could find to pick up and fight with.

The sound of a bugle pierced the mayhem and the rolling thunder of running horses drowned out the sound of the fight. Mason's troop was coming to the rescue, led to the Lopez house by Señor Ruiz.

Bronk, Mason, Boothe and Ugly were slashing with knives and swinging rifles like clubs into the mass of bandits as the fighting became hand to hand. When the mounted troops cleared the corner and entered the street, the surviving bandits turned and ran, but Mason's men rode them down and killed them all with sabers and pistols.

Mason saw El Cuchillo lying on the ground, eyes open. A pistol was in his right hand. El

Cuchillo had blood spurting out of his chest as he breathed his last breaths. Rosa's son, although seriously wounded, kneeled over El Cuchillo and tried to revive his leader. "El Jefe, get up. We will get help."

El Cuchillo looked over towards Mason, then at the boy, "Get a way from me you peasant piece of shit, " then pulled a revolver that he had concealed underneath him and shot Rosa's son between the eyes.

Mason was too weak to move. His ammunition was gone. He stood there helplessly as El Cuchillo turned the pistol towards him, "The same goes for you gringo soldado." Mason and El Cuchillo stared at each other for an instant, then Mason's eyes slowly lifted to a figure behind the prone outlaw. Frank Boothe stood over El Cuchillo with a loaded Colt revolver he recovered from a bandit's body.

"Adios...Pendejo! "

Those were the last words El Cuchillo ever heard as Boothe emptied the gun and blew the outlaw leader's head apart.

Mason pursed his lips and paused. He blinked once and said, "Thank you Corporal Boothe," then collapsed into a sitting position on the ground.

Boothe limped over to Mason. He saw the scout and Bronk walking over too.

They all sat around the Colonel, who was too weak to talk.

Captain DiMarco approached them. He turned and ordered a private to find a doctor.

Mason regained consciousness and smiled at DiMarco, " I never would have guessed they were sending all their men here instead of the exchange House. I wouldn't have left so many of the men scattered out."

DiMarco bit his lip, "Sir, they did hit the exchange house. The men from the 10th are engaging them. They sent a rider to advise us to send support as soon as we could.

Bronk interrupted, "My god, what about our casualties? "

DiMarco looked down, "They were very light... But that's not the end of it." He looked Mason in the eye, "They captured one of the bandits."

"Yes...and?"

"The support they were requesting was for Lieutenant Cleary. At least one hundred riders are attacking the remount corrals as we speak."

Mason's face paled as he strained to get up, "Cleary only has five men. They'll be slaughtered."

DiMarco put his hand on Mason's shoulder, "Sir, you're wounded. We'll organize a rescue."

Mason set his jaw and rose to his feet, "Not

without me you won't. Get me some bandages for my men and have someone bring up our horses. We're moving out in five minutes."

## Chapter 26

Lieutenant Cleary watched as his marksmen cut the approaching enemy down methodically as the Yaqui infantry advanced. The closest man was still over seventy-five yards away. He raised his glasses to the distant group of mounted bandits. He squinted through the binoculars, trying to make out how many of them there were.

"When they come, there will be hell to pay." No one heard him. He saw a group moving over to a flanking position. He gave hand signals to Berkmaier and waited.

The machine gunner moved his barrel towards the group. Cleary knew Berkmaier to be an old Kentucky hunting man. The Lieutenant smiled as he watched Berkmaier lick his thumb then run it across his front sight of his rifle. He made a promise to himself, "These men are getting out of this alive dammit."

He thought he heard some type of explosion in the direction of town.He strained to hear. But didn't detect any further indications of battle.

He laid down the binoculars and picked up his rifle. It was a waiting game now.

Cuatro watched as the two marksmen

decimated the ranks of the Yaquis. He turned to his Sergeant, "Gordo, how much closer do you think the Yaquis can get? "

The fat Sergeant shook his head, I don't know Jefe. I think they are about all in now."

"Watch and learn something Gordo. Those Indians are close. When we charge down the hill, they will attack again. They will get very brave when they see my horsemen coming."

"Yes, Jefe. Then the horses are ours for the taking."

"Tell the men to be prepared. I will give the signal soon."

Pappy Young jumped off his horse lunging toward the explosives. He reached for the fuse, but was too late. The heavy charge of TNT detonated, blowing the front of the exchange house away and instantly vaporizing the big sergeant and his mount.

The soldiers across the street on the rooftops fell back as the buildings shook. The blast created a massive crater in the street that was encircled by dead and wounded men and horses. The stunned survivors staggered down into the crater and began looking for anyone who might have lived through the blast.

The explosion across town shook the ground outside the Lopez home. Colonel Mason steadied himself against his horse, then grabbed a handful of mane and mounted up despite his wounds. He turned the tall thoroughbred towards the border exchange house while giving the order for his soldiers to move out. At the gallop, the small group quickly crossed the town to the main thoroughfare of the border. Even Mason was startled at the sight of the bodies and dead horses strewn down the street. He charged up to to the first soldier he saw, touched the reins, as his horse lowered its backside and skidded to a full stop, "Where is Sergeant Major Young? What happened here?"

The trooper, a young soldier from the Tenth rested his chin on his chest, "He didn't make it Colonel... The bandits... There was a charge planted during the fight. Pappy tried to defuse it. He was too late."

The black trooper looked over to McGuillicotty and saw a tear run down the old sergeant's cheek, leaving a crooked line in the dirt on his face.

"I'm sorry Sergeant Bronk. He tried to save us." The trooper saluted the Colonel, turned, and walked back to the disaster.

"Damn it! " Mason cursed aloud. He spun his

horse toward Captain DiMarco. "Assess what they need here to care for the wounded. Then I need every available man to be ready to ride. You follow us at your best possible speed. We have to get to Cleary."

He looked to Bronk. "Let's finish it."

Bronk looked at the Colonel with the eyes of a dead man. Then he turned his gaze to Boothe and the Scout. "Aye, Colonel... Finish it we will."

The horse soldiers left the town at a high lope.

## Chapter 27

Cleary could tell by the movement in the distance that the mounted outlaws would soon be coming to finish the job the Yaquis started. He watched the flankers moving quickly, then suddenly come to a stop. A quick glance with his field glasses revealed their apparent leader, a tall slender man with his right hand held high. Cleary saw him drop his arm to his side and the flankers moved out at a gallop. Cleary didn't hesitate. He gave Berkmaier a hand signal authorizing him to fire at will. He signaled for the other men to wait.

The lieutenant saw the Yaquis stop and stand up as the horsemen behind them gained momentum. Cleary's jaw tightened. This is it.

The Benet machine gun ripped in waves across the flankers, dropping men and horses by the dozens. A concentrated combination of machine gun and rifle fire drove the attackers off of the flanking positions and back towards the middle with the main assault force.

Berkmaier let loose a rebel howl as he poured it to the bandits, wreaking havoc on their ranks.

Cleary gave the command to commence firing to the remaining troopers, who joined in ripping loose with a deadly volley devastating the horsemen. Men screamed and fell on the gentle slopes approaching the canyon.

Cuatro was taken by surprise again, Cleary thought, He saw the outlaw leader give a signal to fall back and regroup. The few Yaquis left, motivated by the support of the horsemen, continued to move forward on foot. They were unaware that their supporting force was abandoning them to die on the slopes.

The troopers killed off the remaining Yaquis quickly with precisely aimed fire as the attackers stumbled across the rough terrain to close the gap on their prey.

As the last of the Yaquis fell, Cleary gave the command to cease fire. The fight was far from over. They had to conserve ammunition. Cleary surveyed his little command. No casualties... Ammunition supply still in good shape... Maybe, just maybe they could hold out.

He watched as his men continued fortifying their positions, and decided that it would be a good idea to do the same. The time for strategy and planning was now over. The next round of this fight was going to be down and dirty. Cleary picked up his entrenching tool and dug in.

Across the field of battle, Cuatro was mad as hell, "Damn these gringos... Setting an ambush... I should have known they would have more men hidden. How many men did we lose on the last charge Gordo? "

"About twenty or thirty riders and all of the Yaquis," Gordo reported sullenly.

"Pinchi gringo bastards." Cuatro considered just leaving the fight and regrouping with El Cuchillo and the men from the exchange house. However he knew that if they delayed coming back, even more yanqui soldados would be there for them to fight.

Cuatro cursed, "To hell with this. We are going to take those horses and we are going to do it right now."

Cuatro spurred his horse and went to the front of his men, "It's time to make the Gringos pay!" Cuatro's excited horse pranced and reared. He drew a big revolver from a wide leather belt, "Viva Mexico!"

The outlaws cheered and fell into a loose formation behind Cuatro. They charged across the rocky ground towards the mouth of the canyon. The bandits dug into the flanks of the horses with sharp Mexican spurs. Horses ran with wide eyes and flaring nostrils. They were four hundred yards away from the soldiers.

Lieutenant Cleary was out of tricks. This time he knew it would be a blood bath. He loaded all his weapons and laid out his ammunition. He made a last survey of the positions of his men. They were all dug in with decent cover and their positions seemed high enough that the horsemen would have difficulty charging over the top them.

Cleary turned his attention to the enemy and saw an obese outlaw riding towards the front of the pack at three hundred and fifty yards range. Cleary decided if he was going to die, he might as well have some fun first. He looked down the barrel of his '03 and squeezed a round off at the fast moving target... A miss.

He worked the bolt instinctively and tried again at three hundred yards. Softly, he pressed the trigger. He felt the recoil firmly in his shoulder. The shot was good.

He grimly smiled as a fat headless rider led the charge for a few feet before dropping of his horse and flopping onto the ground. "You sons-of - bitches want a fight... Well by God, the Army has one for you."

Cleary heard his riflemen open up. The American soldiers were dropping the bandits quickly. They weren't taking the time to reload. They picked up their extra rifles and poured hellfire into the charging outlaws as fast as possible.

As the bandits hit the two hundred yard range the machine gun opened up again. Berkmaier stitched the mob with burst after fiery burst.

The bandits broke and ran back.

Cuatro was apoplectic with rage. He was down less than forty-five men, yet the gringos still held the canyon. It was their machine gun. Cuatro had to stop the machine gun to get to the horses. He organized his dwindling numbers for another attack.

"Listen to me, hombres. The gringo machine gun is killing our brothers. We are going in again. But this time I want all of you to spread out as widely as possible. That will slow the effectiveness of their machine gun." He pointed at a short older man, "Guillermo, when we charge, take five men and come around the end." Cuatro gestured to the East. "Take out that machine gun from higher ground."

"Yes, Jefe." the older man picked out his men.

Cuatro waved his hat, "Lets go! "

Cleary heard a shout from his machine gunner, "Lieutenant, I'm out of ammunition here."

He cursed to himself and walked towards

Berkmaier's position.

"Private, make the gun inoperable then place it higher in the rocks with your hat."

"Lieutenant, They won't be stupid enough to fall for that will they? "

Cleary smiled, "Never underestimate your enemies capacity for error. Besides, what else can we do?"

Berkmaier nodded and placed the gun as ordered. He picked up a rifle from one of the other soldiers.

They prepared for another assault.

Cleary was very proud of these soldiers. They were preparing for what would most likely be a fight to the death with determination and grit. No one seemed to be scared. At least, no one would allow themselves to show it.

Cleary was too damned mad to be scared. Maybe that's how it works, he thought. If you're fighting a battle like this, then your imminent death is a foregone conclusion. Without that to worry about, a man can get down to doing his job. Let the enemy worry about dying. The young Lieutenant who once held the frontier regulars in disrespect, now realized that there was no place else he would rather serve, no other men he would rather serve with, and no one he could be prouder to die with. He loaded his rifles.

The Mexicans charged again. This time the formation was different. They formed a single line stretched across the entire field of vision. At least twenty-five yards between each rider.

Cleary didn't waste time. He began shooting from the rider to his extreme right and worked his way to the left as they fell. If the soldiers gave the outlaws the opportunity to come up the dry wash and overrun their flank, the fight would soon be over.

The riders rapidly closed the distance to the line, but the American riflemen continued to fire with deadly effect on their numbers. Fifteen more outlaws fell as they approached. The soldiers fought well, but the odds were too great. At fifty yards the bandits still numbered about twenty-five men and were advancing at a blistering gallop. The soldiers drew pistols and prepared for the fight of their lives at point blank range.

Cleary saw Berkmaier empty his weapon as five riders came through the flank. They rode over the top of the disabled machine gun and then charged down through Berkmaier's rifle pit. He stood up swinging his rifle, knocking one rider off a horse; but he was quickly cut down by pistol fire

249

from the others. The rider who was knocked from his horse stood over Berkmaier's body, hacking at it with a machete. Cleary took an aimed rifle shot and killed the bandit with a round through the throat. The four remaining riders charged across the mouth of the canyon. The other soldiers were in better cover than Berkmaier and held off the bandits a few moments longer.

Cleary fixed the bayonet on his rifle as he faced a half a dozen riders charging up the slight rise to his rifle pit. From a kneeling position he shot one in the face with his Colt. Then he killed the horse of another. The horse rolled on the bandit crushing him. The bandit wasn't killed instantly, but lay under the dead horse thrashing and screaming as blood ran out his eyes, ears, and mouth.

Lieutenant Cleary grabbed his rifle and thrust a bayonet into the side of the closest rider. A butt stroke dropped the next one.

Cleary knew he was shot through the stomach and shoulder by pistol fire, but he only noticed a burning sensation. The rage of a battle to the death overwhelmed the instinct to respond to pain.

The Lieutenant ran down the gentle slope with his Springfield. Thrusting with the bayonet when a rider got close enough. No time to reload and shoot. He was hit again in the leg. He stumbled.

A bandit rode behind Cleary and clubbed him on the head with an empty pistol. The Lieutenant fell to the ground stunned. He rolled over and pulled his other Colt out of his belt and blasted the bandit out of the saddle. He forced himself to his feet, and staggered back into the canyon. Another wounded soldier made it back with him as they retreated to the cover of a large boulder. The bandits appeared to be riding in confusion. They killed the other remaining soldiers on the slopes as they rode chaotically into the mouth of the canyon.

Cleary checked his ammo. Four rounds in the Colt. He looked at the Trooper he knew only as Private Irwin. Irwin shook his head and held up two fingers.

The Lieutenant smiled and put his hand on Irwin's shoulder, "Save the last round for..."

"Ourselves?" Irwin asked.

"No... use every last round on these filthy bastards," Clearly said with a nasty grin. "Make 'em earn it."

Irwin grimly smiled back and pulled a bowie knife out of his belt, "Yes, sir... I ain't done yet. "

Cuatro determined that only a couple of the soldiers were left. He stopped at the mouth of the canyon to deal with them. Stepping down off his horse, he gave terms of surrender, "Soldiers. Give up and we will spare you. Come on out. There is no sense dying for a lost cause."

Cleary stepped out from behind the boulder. Irwin stepped out from the other side. The Lieutenant stared Cuatro in the eyes. Cuatro laughed nervously, "Throw down your guns. I command you to surrender or die. Do you hear me? Your cause is lost."

As Cuatro spoke, the twenty remaining bandits sat on horseback at Cuatro's sides, guns drawn.

The Lieutenant let an uncomfortable silence grate on the nerves of the bandits before he spoke, "Your right, outlaw... There is no sense dying for a lost cause."

Cuatro sneered with arrogance at his defeated enemy.

Cleary spit a mouthful of blood on the ground, "But nobody will ever accuse you of being sensible! " Cleary snap fired the Colt striking Cuatro in the stomach with a massive .45 caliber round.

Cuatro lurched forward as the wind was sucked out of his lungs by the impact. A bizarre silence lingered as the stunned bandits stared at the soldier then their leader.

Cuatro gasped for air. The soldiers didn't move. Cuatro's tortured breaths made a sickening rasping sound. The bandit leader straightened himself, his right arm holding his midsection. With his left hand he slowly raised his pistol.

The silence was suddenly broken by a piercing sound.... A bugle call.

Irwin whispered, "Mason! "

Cuatro squeezed the trigger of his pistol, shooting Cleary in the chest as the bandit fell off his horse.

Panic consumed the remaining bandits. They opened fire on Irwin but the game soldier returned fire with his last two rounds.

A pistol round from the bandits creased his scalp and he went down.

Not wanting to be trapped, the surviving outlaws made a run for it out of the mouth of the box canyon and ran head on into a United States Cavalry pistol charge.

Mason drew his saber and spurred his mount. Although his strength had been diminished by his wounds, he led the charge with pure rage carrying him forward.

Boothe let go of his reins and drew pistols. His mount stayed in formation as they closed the gap between themselves and the retreating bandits.

Using only knee pressure, he guided the big horse
to the closest enemy, and fired at point blank
range blasting the outlaw out of the saddle.

Bronk headed off a rider that tried to turn
away from the rest of the band. He gave Mac his
head and the husky Morgan ran his chest into the
side of the escaping rider's mount knocking them
all to the ground . The bandit got up with a
machete in his hand. He took a swipe at Bronk, but
the old soldier ducked under it and shot the bandit
in the knee.

The outlaw fell backwards, screaming in pain.
The screams were quickly muffled as Bronk fell on
top of him, grabbing the bandit by the throat with
both hands and crushing his windpipe. Then he
smashed the bandits head against the rocky
ground for good measure, before getting to his
feet.

The mounted engagement was short. The
bandits attempted to scatter but were run down
by the enraged cavalry soldiers. Thirsting for
revenge, the troopers took no prisoners. They
littered the high desert with the bodies of fleeing
outlaws.

The confrontation now ended, the troopers
cleared the canyon on foot, carefully scouring

every rock and hiding place for survivors. The soldiers were sickened by the mutilated bodies of their comrades as they found them. Berkmaier had been hacked up badly, with what must have been a sword or machete. The men found near their rifle pits were obviously shot and stabbed numerous times after their death.

Along the rim of the canyon wall, another trooper provided cover as he searched. Trooper Darden edged along at point taking the high ground. Darden was a different man than he had been earlier that day. He had seen his leader and hero, Pappy Young, killed in action. Many of his friends were killed too. The sad part for him was that this was not a real war with a noble cause, a war against an aggressor nation. His friends had simply been murdered in the desert by vicious criminals, fanatical bandits with no real home or loyalties. Darden found a position where he could see some activity near a boulder at the base of the canyon. He wiped across his eyes with his sleeve, "Somebody is going to pay."

Cleary barely had the strength left to open his eyes. The rage had left him. Now he felt only pain. He was getting cold. He tried to focus but saw only shadows. He heard the bandits voice.

"Soldado. You shot me you bastard."

The lieutenant saw a figure pointing at him through a haze. He wasn't certain if he was dreaming or if it was real. Then he heard the hammer of a single action revolver being pulled back and the rotation of the cylinder as it locked into place.

"You die, bastard."

From his position in the rocks, Trooper Darden could see the Mexican bandit standing over a wounded trooper. He raised his Springfield. "You die, bastard."

The lieutenant could no longer see, he was blinded from his wounds. But he heard the report of a rifle. He felt a warm spray on his face, then he heard the muffled sound of something falling to the ground. He wanted to sleep. He was so cold.

McGuillicotty and Boothe helped Mason off his horse. The wounds of the day's battles were taking a heavy toll on him. The men and horses were exhausted. The trooper and sergeant supported the Colonel and led him to the back of the canyon near a large boulder. Mason saw Trooper Darden tending to the fallen Lieutenant Cleary.

It was obvious. Clearly was dying… many of the wounds he sustained were mortal in and of themselves. He had no hope of survival.

Darden looked up as the three men approached and sadly shook his head. Mason fought back tears as he knelt beside the fallen young officer. Cleary appeared to have been wounded at least six times, his uniform shredded and soaked in blood.

Bronk couldn't hold back his grief as he held Cleary's hand. The big Sergeant wept.

Frank Boothe closed his eyes and prayed. When he opened them again the young lieutenant was gone. Cleary never regained consciousness. He never had a chance to share a final sentiment. He died in the Colonel's arms.

Other troopers carried out Irwin. He was still alive, the lone survivor. Mason, McGuillicotty, and Boothe walked out of the canyon with the living.

"We paid dearly today, Bronk " Mason wet his lips and wiped his face with his sleeve.

"Aye, sir, that we did."

Frank stopped and looked across the horizon, " Is that the end of it? "

Colonel Mason gazed sadly with him at the high desert of Arizona, " Not for us son. Not by a long shot."

*Daniel Byram*

# Epilogue

### Outside Fort Huachuca - 1951

The old man took a sip of his tea. "When Irwin recovered, he told us of how courageous Lieutenant Cleary had been in the battle. It was a very sad thing. He was a fine man. He would have been an outstanding officer."

The Corporal sat down his pencil, "What happened to the rest of them? Was there more fighting? What about the punitive expedition? How come I've never heard of this?

The old man gave a faint smile and raised his hand to settle the excited young soldier, "There is more... but not today, young man. Please remember our agreement."

"May I come back again, sir... I'd like to hear more."

"Come back next week if you wish. But it might cost you another favor."

The young man put his notepad and pencil under his arm and walked to the door. He paused and turned. He looked into the eyes of the old man in the rocking chair. He snapped to attention and saluted. "Thank you, Colonel Mason. I won't forget."

The old warrior slowly raised himself from the

chair and returned the salute, "That's all I ask."

Douglas Arizona - 1951

The little girl found the bouquet on the sidewalk near the border. There was no card. She picked the flowers up and waited in front of the bank building for her mom. She leaned against the bronze plaque that said something about a historical site.

No one would ever find the other flowers left in the remote box canyon in Cochise County. The soldier set them down near a mound of rocks. He pulled a metal flask from his coat and drank a toast, "To absent companions, you will not be forgotten."

TILL OUR NEXT POSTING...
The End

## Historical References:

Although the characters and events in this story are fictional, the reader may enjoy knowing that there are historical aspects to the story of the troopers of Cochise County, Arizona.

— Camp Harry Jones was located in Douglas, Arizona at the turn of the century until its closure in the 1930's. It was originally called Camp Douglas. Harry Jones was a trooper who was killed while tending horses by a stray bullet fired by Mexican bandits across the border.

— The John Slaughter Ranch in San Bernardino Valley, east of Douglas on the border still exists and is open to visitors today. Sheriff Slaughter was a great supporter of the military and the stone foundations of an Army outpost near his ranch headquarters can be seen on the property. He had one of the first automobiles in Cochise County but he never learned to drive. His friend and assistant, a former slave known as 'Old Bat' and a Chinese cook known as John Lee May were real people, his friends who lived at the ranch with him. The ranch is still open to visitors and is one of the best kept secrets of Arizona historical sights.

— Rurales captured a young officer based out

of Camp Jones after he unintentionally strolled across the border while hunting birds during a patrol in the San Bernardino Valley. His Sergeant led an unauthorized charge into Mexico and rescued his wandering commander. They killed at least two of the Rurales according to some accounts, and captured the rest of them. The prisoners were held at the camp for while as the United States and the Government of Mexico both ignored the situation. Eventually, the camp commander unilaterally sent the prisoners home to Mexico *(although it was reliably reported they wanted to stay at the camp)*.

    –   The Buffalo Soldiers were an active part of the border defense of the United States. They were based in Fort Huachuca and served gallantly in many border confrontations, skirmishes, and in the Punitive Expedition. The museum at Fort Huachuca has a great deal of interesting information about this famous troop.

    –   The last group of Apache Scouts served in Cochise County, some of them serving honorably for over 40 years. There is also a great deal of information available about them in the Fort Huachuca Museum.

    –   A heroic Arizona Ranger was gunned down by vengeful outlaws on the Mexican side of the border near Naco. He was recognized in a cantina by outlaws he had past dealings with. The outlaws opened fire on the ranger. Although severely wounded, he tried to crawl to the border as the outlaws continued to shoot him in the back, but never made it as he died only feet away from the United States.

– Border outlaws made numerous raids on the ranches, towns, and cities in Cochise county.

– The battlefield rescue described in the prologue was based on a battle in which the Buffalo Soldiers and soldiers of the regular Army, were intermixed with volunteer Rough Riders as command structures and organization went into disarray during the Cuban Campaign.

–The fictional battle of Crosswinds Canyon in the final chapters of this book was inspired by the story of a brave young Lieutenant Howard B. Cushing who lost his life in a battle with the Chiricahua Apaches in the Whetstone Mountains May 5, 1871 while leading a small group of cavalrymen. Quick thinking by Sergeant John Mott resulted in the survival of a few of the men after Lieutenant Cushing was killed.

*Daniel Byram*

## Acknowledgements

I would like to thank Ted Jones of Rem's Farm Saddlery for use of photographs of the McClellan Saddle and the Heart Breast Collar.

My sincere appreciation to Jan Hancock, author of Horse Trails of Arizona, for taking the time to provide me with additional details about camping with horses in Cochise County. Her book is required reading for all Arizona trail riders.

*Daniel Byram*

# Research locations

## Fort Huachuca

The fort has a beautiful parade ground and an excellent museum with significant displays referencing the history of the horse soldiers. The nearby cemetery is also well worth visiting. Horse cavalry enthusiasts might inquire about B Troop, the fort's re-enactment group.

## Downtown Douglas, Arizona

The Douglas, historic business district features buildings designed and built from 1905 to 1920

## Historic residences of Douglas

The residences located roughly between 7th to 12 Street, and Carmelita to E Avenue, were built between 1905 and 1925 in varying styles included Period Revival, Queen Anne, and bungalow.

## Sonoran style row houses

These interesting and historical structures can be found near H and I Avenues by 6th street and 9th street

## Douglas Williams House

Built in 1909 this beautiful house is the home of the Douglas Historical Society. It is located on the Northeast corner of 10th Street and D Avenue

## San Bernardino Ranch

The historic home of the famous lawman John Slaughter is located 18 miles east of Douglas on a well maintained gravel road.

## Auga Prieta, Mexico

The twin city to Douglas, Arizona has shopping, restaurants, and night clubs.

## Tombstone, Arizona

Attendance is mandatory for anyone visiting Cochise County. Have a great time... Wyatt Earp... Clantons... Tombstone Epitaph... Buckskin Frank Leslie... Bat Masterson... enough said

## Gadsden Hotel

The hotel is located at 1046 G Avenue in Douglas, Arizona. It is worth a visit to see the 42 foot tall stained glass mural.

The Gadsden was designed by architect H.C.

Frost in 1907. The original structure was destroyed in a fire in 1927 and was rebuilt the following year. They prefer that you don't ride your horse into the lobby.

*Daniel Byram*

# Resources

## A list of works consulted

Bourke, John. On the Border with Crook. Omaha: University of Nebraska Press, 1971

Erwin, Allen A. The Southwest of John Slaughter 1841 to1922. Glendale, California. Arthur Clark - Publisher. Glendale, California 1965

Miller, Joseph. The Arizona Rangers. New York. Hastings House. 1972

Smith, Cornelius C. Jr. Fort Huachuca. The Story of a Frontier Post. Washington DC. US Government Printing Office. 1976.

Steffen, Randy. The Horse Soldiers 1776 -1943. University of Oklahoma Press. 1978.

Truscott, Lucian K. Jr. The Twilight of the US Cavalry. Life in the Old Army 1917 -1942. Lawrence , Kansas. University Press of Kansas. 1989.

Warfield, H.B. 10th Cavalry and Border Fights. Wells, Reba B. The San Bernardino Ranch.

Douglas, Arizona. The Cochise Quarterly. 1985

Wells, Reba B. <u>Slaughter Ranch Outpost</u>.
Douglas, Arizona. The Cochise Quarterly 1985

## About the author

Daniel Byram is a retired Arizona Peace Officer. During his years in command of a special investigation unit, he dealt first-hand with the modern version of border outlaws and cut-throats. He applied some of his experiences to the development of this story. While researching this book he rode throughout the areas described in the story on his pinto horse Dakota.

He has since moved to California where he started a successful technology company. He is semi-retired and living in Coronado. He spends his time aboard his boat, the Wandering Star, or at the beach.

www.ingramcontent.com/pod-product-compliance
Lightning Source LLC
Chambersburg PA
CBHW031300170626
46807CB00001B/233